‘‘It’s hardly likely I’ll fall in love.’’

Lucas laughed as he went on. ‘‘I have myself well under control—too much to allow myself to become besotted as I once was—’’

‘‘I doubt that you’ve ever been besotted over anyone. It was only your ego that suffered . . .’’ The words faded to a whisper as Sylvia recalled his aunt’s words. *I was really worried about him,* she’d declared.

And then a mixture of sympathy and guilt, coupled with something she was unable to control, caused her to raise her face to brush his lips with her own. ‘‘I’m sorry for having hurt you to that extent,’’ she said in a low voice.

‘‘Then kiss me again to prove it.’’

The words came in a tense command and she lifted her face without hesitation. . . .

Miriam MacGregor began writing under the tutelage of a renowned military historian, and produced articles, books—fiction and nonfiction—concerning New Zealand's pioneer days, as well as plays for a local drama club. In 1984 she received an award for her contribution to New Zealand's literary field. She now writes romance novels exclusively and derives great pleasure from offering readers escape from everyday life. She and her husband live on a sheep-and-cattle station near the small town of Waipawa.

Books by Miriam MacGregor

HARLEQUIN ROMANCE

2710—BOSS OF BRIGHTLANDS
2733—SPRING AT SEVENOAKS
2794—CALL OF THE MOUNTAIN
2823—WINTER AT WHITECLIFFS
2849—STAIRWAY TO DESTINY
2890—AUTUMN AT AUBREY'S
2931—RIDER OF THE HILLS
2996—LORD OF THE LODGE
3022—RIDDELL OF RIVERMOON
3060—MAN OF THE HOUSE

CARVILLE'S CASTLE

Miriam MacGregor

Harlequin Books

TORONTO • NEW YORK • LONDON
AMSTERDAM • PARIS • SYDNEY • HAMBURG
STOCKHOLM • ATHENS • TOKYO • MILAN

Original hardcover edition published in 1990
by Mills & Boon Limited

ISBN 0-373-03083-5

Harlequin Romance first edition October 1990

Printed in U.S.A.

CHAPTER ONE

SYLVIA'S nerves tingled as she left her small blue Honda Civic in the parking area, then walked along the Rotorua street. The vague odour of sulphur wafting from the city's thermal areas heralded rain, while the coolness of the New Zealand spring morning caused her to fasten the buttons of her jacket.

As she drew near to her destination her tenseness increased, but whether its cause rose from nervousness or excitement she was unable to define. At the same time she told herself that a mixture of both sensations was permissible when about to begin the first day in a new job—and especially in a new job such as this one.

'It's in Mr Carville's accountancy office,' the woman in the employment agency had informed her. 'So much influenza raging in the city—it's been necessary for him to send us an emergency call.'

'You mean—*Lucas Carville*?' Sylvia bit her lip, then swallowed.

'Yes. His rise to success has been surprisingly rapid. You'll be doing computer work most of the time.'

Sylvia had remained perfectly still, staring down at the card giving her the address of Lucas Carville's office. Was she wise to accept this job? she wondered. Or would it entail the embarrassment of opening old wounds? She had only to hand the card back to the woman and ask if she had anything else on her books. But she had not done so because questions would be asked—questions she had no wish to answer.

Shivering slightly, she began to wonder if the chill in the September air could be an omen of the reception she could expect from Lucas Carville. However, with luck he wouldn't even remember her. After all, it was seven years since she had last seen him—seven years since she'd told him she hoped she'd never set eyes on him again.

Yes, with luck he'd have completely forgotten her existence, although she knew that, deep down, she had never quite forgotten him. Somewhere within the darkest recess of her mind he had continued to hover like a spectre with a pained expression—a ghost that had been hurt by her.

She reached a doorway with a polished brass plate set beside it, the words stating that these were the offices of Lucas Carville, Chartered Accountant. Behind the doorway stretched a single-storeyed building constructed on lines of modern architecture.

Sylvia paused, staring at the name on the plate and thinking of Lucas as he'd been when she had first known him. At that time he had been twenty-three, and six years older than her own age of seventeen. He had been a serious young man, far too solemn for her taste at that period of her life, and with absolutely no *fizz* about him, her girlish mind had decided. Those were the days when she had been searching for someone with whom to have fun, rather than a staid man who was wrapped in the study of economics.

And then Brian had appeared. Brian Brookes had been full of gaiety and laughter, and Lucas had been given short shrift. Brian had been taken into her father's land agency business, while Lucas had departed for Auckland to further his experience in the accountancy world. Since then she had had her wish of not setting eyes on him again.

Since those days Sylvia's outlook had changed. Her father had died and her feet had been brought down to earth with a thud. She had also learnt that fun and fizz were not the most important things in life, and that love, coupled with stability, held a high place in the scheme of things.

In short, she had matured. She had grown up. She was no longer the same flibbertigibbet of seven years ago. 'Flighty' was the word Lucas had flung at her, she now recalled with a tinge of embarrassment. A girl who led men on, then turned her back. But she had not been like that, she defended mentally. It had been Lucas who had taken too much for granted.

Brushing the memories aside, she went towards the reception desk, to be faced by two girls younger than herself. They looked at her with interest as she smiled and introduced herself.

'I'm Sylvia Sinclair. I've come to work here.'

The elder girl had short dark hair and brown eyes that smiled as she spoke. 'Hi— I'm Karen, and this is June. We were told the employment agency was sending somebody to help out while Ransom—I mean while *Miss* Ransom is away. She's our senior and is quite ill with 'flu. The boss is in a real flap without her.'

Sylvia felt a wave of disappointment. 'Help out? Are you saying the job is only a temporary one?'

'That will depend upon whether both Miss Ransom—and the boss, of course—find you satisfactory. I do most of the typing, but how are you on all this high technology? We really need an expert on the extra computer that's sitting idle.'

'I dare say I'll cope with it.'

'In that case you'd better go in and see the boss. Give him a buzz, June.'

The younger girl had fair straight hair with a tinge of red in it. She wore it pushed behind her ears, with a fringe that fell across her brows. A few words were spoken on the office intercom, then she turned to Sylvia. 'He'll see you now. Go down that passage. It's the last door on the right.' She giggled, then added in a whisper, 'We call him Mr Fantastic!'

Sylvia took a deep breath, then made her way along the passage. She passed closed doors, her feet making no sound on the thick red carpet, and as she went beyond a collection of potted plants she thought, this is it. Give him one minute of memory flashback and I'll be out on my ear. Huh—Mr Fantastic, indeed!

The man who stood up as she entered his office was above average height. He was easily recognisable as the Lucas she had known during earlier years, except that there was a definite change about him. He was older, of course, although he still retained his athletic form, yet in some mysterious way he had developed into one of the most handsome men she had ever seen.

She knew that his dark eyes surveyed her with a penetrating scrutiny, and she wondered if her nervousness had become obvious. However, he gave no sign of recognition, and she then realised his interest appeared to have become centred on her hair, following its shining blonde length from the crown of her head to the ends curling about her shoulders.

He spoke quietly, his voice deep, 'You're Miss Sinclair?'

'Yes. And you are Mr Carville?' For Pete's sake, didn't he recognise her? Why this play-acting? Was it his idea of a joke? The situation made her feel slightly hysterical.

His face remained serious. 'The agency said you're accustomed to computer work.'

'That's right. I have references.' Sylvia took papers from her shoulderbag and passed them across the shining mahogany desk, then, while he examined them, she averted her eyes from his face by staring at the books and stacks of papers on the shelves behind his head.

At last he shot a question at her. 'What happened to your old job?'

'The place closed down. I was made redundant along with several other people.' Her blue eyes clouded as she realised the difficulty some of them would have in finding other jobs. The thought made her say, 'I believe your Miss Ransom is ill.'

'That's right. She wasn't well last Friday, so I told her to stay away until she's completely better, or at least until there's no fear of her putting 'flu through the entire office. There's so much of it about, and it upsets the work routine.'

'Does that mean this job is just a temporary one until she returns?'

'Not necessarily. Maureen needs an assistant because the load on her shoulders is becoming rather heavy. If you get on well together you'll find the job is permanent.'

So her job depended on Maureen, she thought. Aloud she said, 'Karen doesn't do computer work?'

'Her place is at the typewriter. I must have someone to take care of correspondence. As for young June, she's the receptionist who answers the phone, makes the tea and is also given other tasks. I can assure you it's a busy office.'

Sylvia looked at him, still waiting for a sign of recognition, but it did not come. Surely she herself hadn't changed to that extent? Or was he conveying the fact that she'd been completely wiped from his mind? If so, he was doing it most successfully.

Feeling nettled, she said, 'Well, if you'll give me a few directions I'll make a start on whatever needs the most attention.'

'Right. Come this way.' He led her out into the passage, then indicated one of its doors. 'That's the girls' room. There's a hanger for your jacket and a locker you can use.'

She knew he stood waiting in the passage while she divested herself of her jacket, and she felt thankful she'd worn her conservative navy blue suit with its knife-pleated skirt and frilled pale pink blouse which softened it and gave it a feminine touch.

A quick glance in the mirror showed her face to be slightly flushed, while the navy reflected her eyes, making them look like dark blue pansies. The sight of them caused her to catch her breath as memory flooded her mind. Wasn't that what Lucas called her so long ago? *Pansy eyes.*

She hurried out to the passage again and he led her to another room where samples of modern technology presented keyboards and screens, and, indicating a pile of papers beside one of them, he said, 'Perhaps you'll be able to continue where Maureen left off.' Further details of the work being done were explained, then he asked, 'Do you understand how to work this type of machine?'

'Yes—it's not a stranger to me.' And thank heavens for that, she added silently to herself.

'Then you shouldn't find it too difficult.'

'Not at all.'

'I must say it'll be a relief to see the work continue, so I'll leave you to get on with it.' He paused, then asked, 'Have you made arrangements for lunch?'

The question surprised her. 'Lunch? No.'

'Then we'll lunch together and you can tell me a little about yourself.' The words carried the tone of an order.

Sylvia looked at him in bewildered silence. Had he recognised her after all?

But his next words seemed to belie this suspicion. 'I like to know a little about my employees. If I know of their problems at home it helps to give better understanding at work.'

'I see.' Was this his real reason? she wondered. Or did it mean he meant to ply her with questions? If so, he'd soon recall his earlier association with her, brief as it had been. She had only to tell him where she lived and his memory would be jolted into remembering their home in Sophia Street.

She worked steadily until ten o'clock when June came to tell her it was time for morning break. 'We have tea in what we call the kitchen, although Mr Carville has his in his office,' the younger girl said as she led the way to a back room which had tea-making facilities, washing-up sink, a cupboard and small fridge.

Karen pulled a stool from beneath the bench. 'You may have lunch here if you like,' she said as she offered it to Sylvia. 'Miss Ransom often does if she's extra busy.'

June smiled wickedly. 'Or if she thinks there's any chance of being taken out to lunch——'

'Shut up, June,' Karen snapped. Then to Sylvia, 'There's a good restaurant not far from here. You can get takeaways like hot pies, sandwiches or croissants.'

Sylvia smiled. 'Thank you, but it won't be necessary today. Mr Carville has said I'm to lunch with him.'

Their eyes widened. *'Lunch?'* Karen exclaimed. 'Are you saying Mr Fantastic is taking you to lunch—so *soon*?'

'It's just a matter of getting to know me as a new member of the staff,' Sylvia explained in an offhand manner.

'Cor——!' June's voice had become hushed.

'It's probably one of his habits,' Sylvia suggested, casually sipping her tea.

'Like smoke, it is,' Karen retorted. 'I've never known him to take staff to lunch. Poor old Ransom's been trying to wangle an invitation ever since I've been here.'

'Miss Ransom is elderly?' queried Sylvia.

'Ancient. She must be edging thirty at least,' June supplied.

'But you can't deny she's rather good-looking,' Karen declared. 'She's got grey eyes that sort of darken with flecks of brown, specially when she's mad about something. She opens them wide when *he's* around!'

'And she's got light brown hair that gets a golden gleam when the sun shines on it,' added June.

Karen looked at Sylvia with a speculative glint in her eyes. 'I'll bet it's your blonde hair that's caught his fancy. Some men are positive suckers for blondes. Is it bleached?'

Sylvia shook her head. 'There's no need, thank goodness.'

Karen giggled. 'The Ransom bleached hers for a while, but it didn't work in getting her taken out to lunch.'

'That's right,' June exclaimed, her eyes alive with recollection. 'And then she tried it with blonde streaks, but that didn't work either.' She gave an exaggerated sigh. 'Poor old Ransom, she just can't pin him down, despite the exams she seems to have passed.'

Sylvia found herself feeling sympathetic towards the absent office senior who seemed to be known as 'the Ransom' to these two incorrigibles. As she put her cup down the younger of them said, 'Don't bother to wash it. I attend to the kitchen chores and make sure we have biscuits in the tin.'

Sylvia smiled. 'You do? Thank you, June. You also make a good cup of tea. Now I'd better get back to the computer. I'm anxious to have something to show for the morning's work.'

As she went towards the door Karen waylaid her by placing a hand on her arm. 'May I offer a small piece of advice?'

Sylvia's brows rose. 'Yes, of course.'

'When the Ransom comes back to work I wouldn't tell her you've been to lunch with *him*.'

Sylvia sent glances from one to the other, a faint smile hovering about her lips. 'Something tells me it won't be long before the news reaches her ears.'

Karen's air became one of injury. 'Are you suggesting we'll tell her? You're so sure one of us will blab?'

'It really doesn't matter if you do,' Sylvia replied quietly. 'I have a strong suspicion that my days here will not last for very long. In fact, they're already numbered.'

Their eyes were full of curiosity. 'Why do you say that?' June queried.

But Sylvia made no answer as she hurried back to her office, where she worked steadily until midday. Then she went across the passage to the girls' room where she ran a comb through her hair and attended to her make-up. Then, slipping her arms into her jacket, she went out into the passage.

He was waiting for her, tall and debonair, his dark grey business suit fitting perfectly across his broad shoulders, the red in his silk tie and matching breast pocket handkerchief adding a touch of colour to the sombre shade. In a subtle way he oozed success, and this was emphasised as he led her to the parking area at the back of the offices to where a white Alfa Romeo stood waiting.

Moments later they were driving towards Fenton Street, where they turned right to follow the road that would take them out of the city. There was silence while they passed numerous motels, the racecourse, and as they drew nearer the Sophia Street turn-off Sylvia held her breath.

Did he intend to drive along its length of tree-sheltered homes and perhaps stop at her own? Was it his intention to tell her to get out of the car, to go back to her own pad and stay there, and that he hoped he'd never set eyes on her again—just as she'd once told him? How could he have forgotten?

And then she breathed more freely again, because he passed Sophia Street without comment and was heading towards the weird Whaka-rewa-rewa thermal area with its steam rising on all sides and where the Pohutu geyser flung itself at least sixty feet into the air.

Did he intend to take a pre-lunch walk along the paths where pools bubbled with boiling water, porridge pot mud plopped or leapt into the air like frogs springing from one place to another? Years ago they had walked along those paths. *Surely he remembered?*

Tentatively Sylvia asked, 'Do you ever walk round Whaka?'

'Only when I have out-of-town clients who haven't seen the place or who would like to take another look at it.'

'Oh.' She waited to hear more.

'And then I have Australian friends who make the odd trip across the Tasman. Most of them know I own a house and are welcome to pay a visit.'

Sylvia frowned, trying to recall his previous circumstances, but had no recollection of them including a house. And then she remembered Lucas had lived with his grandfather, although she had never seen the house or met the old man. Their short association had ended before that could happen.

To prevent further lapses into silence, she asked, 'You've spent a period in Australia?'

'Yes. I worked in Sydney for a few years until circumstances brought me back to Rotorua.'

'Oh? When was that?'

'Three years ago, during which time I've been busy. Nose to the grindstone, you understand.'

Sylvia stared straight ahead. It was strange that she hadn't heard of his return, she thought. Yet not so strange when she considered that she herself had spent a few years working in Auckland, and during that time she had really lost track of what was going on in Rotorua.

She had sought a job in Auckland to get away from Brian, whose attentions had become overbearing. The fact that he had become part of her father's land agency business made him imagine he had a proprietorial right over herself. In Auckland her knowledge of office equipment had advanced, and then her father's death had caused her to return to Rotorua to be with her mother.

She came out of her nostalgia to glance about her. Lucas had driven beyond the steaming area of Whaka-rewa-rewa and was now heading towards open country where sheep and cattle grazed the fresh spring pastures. She remained silent until they passed Rainbow Mountain with its patches of colour and its afforestation, then she turned to him with a question. 'Where are we going?'

'To the tea-room at Waiotapu.' The reply came nonchalantly.

Waiotapu. The realisation that she was being taken there came as a shock. In the Maori language the name meant sacred waters. In her own language it was the place where their previous relationship had ended.

She recalled watching the Lady Knox geyser send its high plume into the air, and it was here that Lucas's fingers had found her own. She had removed them gently, and they had walked between the many colourful craters, some of them with deep rumblings within their depths.

At the Artist's Palette with its steaming fumeroles and boiling mud in an amazing variety of colours, and also while standing beside the golden edge of the Champagne Pool, Lucas had again taken her hand, and once more she had removed it. However, it was not until they had reached the Bridal Veil Falls that the real quarrel had occurred.

Thinking about the incident, Sylvia hardly noticed the miles slip by until a sign announced the Waiotapu Thermal Wonderland. On the left the hills were tree-covered, while near the roadside steam rose lazily to waft through the green branches. However, Lucas did not turn off the highway to follow the winding road to the Waiotapu parking area. Instead he pulled in to where a tea-room stood on the right-hand side of the road, its bareness softened by a few flowering shrubs.

Sylvia was not sure whether she was relieved or assailed by a feeling of anticlimax. 'It'll be a long lunch hour—and with so much work to be done,' she murmured.

'Sometimes I have a desire for relaxation,' he told her.

Relaxation? He expected her to relax? she questioned mentally.

They walked past bins of fresh fruit, then went into the shop where groceries were sold. A divider gave access to the dining-room, where sandwiches, cakes, cream buns and bread rolls were attractively presented in glass-fronted cabinets.

Sylvia chose very little food. She had begun to feel uncomfortable and was vaguely conscious of a feeling of foreboding which caused her appetite to disappear. At the same time she watched Lucas Carville fill his plate, while the smile playing about his lips made her suspect he was secretly enjoying himself.

He led her to a window from where they could see the steam rising from the trees across the road. Cars turned off the highway to disappear towards the Wonderland parking area, and again Sylvia recalled the last time she had been there. She then became aware that Lucas was leaning back in his chair, regarding her quizzically.

'Well now, tell me about yourself,' he said.

Her shoulders lifted in the slightest of shrugs. 'There's nothing to tell.'

'Everyone has something to tell.'

'Does that mean you yourself have plenty to relate—Mr Carville?'

'Are you sending the ball back into my court—Miss Sinclair?'

At that moment one of the tea-room staff came to their table with a tray holding two glasses and a small decanter of sherry. 'Compliments of the boss, Mr Carville,' she said.

Lucas grinned at her. 'Thank you. Please convey my gratitude.'

'You must be well-known here,' Sylvia observed.

'I suppose you could say so. I often bring a guest for a quick bite and a rapid look round the thermal area.'

But so far not the Ransom, she thought, then glanced about her. The dining-room was spotlessly clean, although it leaned towards being slightly shabby. The floral material covering the wire-backed chairs was faded, while the chocolate-brown carpet was becoming worn.

Turning to him, she remarked, 'It's not the most swept-up place to bring guests.'

His eyes held her own as he explained, 'They're brought here for a purpose.'

She felt a rising apprehension. Had she been brought here for a purpose—perhaps to be relentlessly subjected to memories of the past? Controlling her nerves, she said, 'Naturally, if they're strangers to Rotorua they'd find Waiotapu quite fascinating.'

'That's right.'

Suddenly she felt unable to meet his eyes. Was it her imagination that he watched her intently, or was it just that his dark eyes were as penetrating as ever?

He returned to his former subject by repeating his request. 'So—tell me about yourself. Have you spent all your life in Rotorua?'

'No. I had a period in Auckland.'

'What brought you back to Rotorua? A boyfriend, no doubt?'

'No. It was my father's death. He had a massive coronary and I felt I should be with my mother.'

'But there must be a boyfriend tucked away somewhere, although I see no engagement ring. You're not *walking out*?' he queried facetiously, using an old-time expression.

'You mean *keeping company*?' she quipped back. 'Indeed no, sir—I'm much too busy in the evenings and at the weekends.'

'Doing what?' The dark eyes continued to regard her intently.

'Helping my mother.' She hesitated, then explained, 'After my father's death Mother felt she had to put her mind to something. She was a nurse before she married and until I was born, so now she's turned our home into a convalescent place. She takes in people who need assistance after being ill. Sometimes people have no one to care for them when they leave hospital, so they come to Mother until they feel stronger.'

'A most worthy project, by the sound of it. She has help?'

'Yes. She has Wiki, a Maori woman who comes in each day, but who has her weekends free. Mother says she couldn't manage without Wiki.'

'What is your part in this scheme?' He was looking at her hands.

'I give Mother a break in the evenings—unless somebody is there she refuses to go out and leave them. However, I've now persuaded her to join a social club which enables her to be among people who aren't just getting over illness.'

'Does this mean that you yourself seldom go out? Are you saying you stay at home every evening?'

'Certainly not!' Sylvia declared with indignation. 'Do I look like a hermit?'

'No hermit could be so attractive.' His eyes were taking in details, moving from her blonde hair to her deep blue eyes with their dark lashes that cast shadows on her cheeks. The curve of her sweet lips came in for a lingering scrutiny, and from there his gaze moved to her neck where the ruffles of her pale pink blouse nestled against her throat. And then his next words startled her.

'I presume you're—unattached?'

'You mean—engaged?' Sylvia displayed her left hand. 'Do you see a ring on my finger?'

'It could be an invisible one.'

'I don't understand.'

'A girl doesn't need a ring to be tied. A close association can be sufficient.'

She sent a fleeting thought towards Brian, then shook her head as she said, 'Not engaged, nor likely to be.'

'Allergic to men?'

'Not at all. I just like to be free.'

Lucas gave a short laugh. 'That makes two of us.'

She hesitated, then asked, 'You're admitting to being—unattached?'

'That's right.' He glanced at the expensive gold watch covering the dark hairs on his wrist. 'I suppose we'd better return to the office.'

'Yes, there's work to be done, and we've spent so much time here.'

'Otherwise I'd walk you round Waiotapu—especially to the Bridal Veil Falls.' He sent her a searching look as he uttered the last words.

Her heart skipped a beat, her confidence draining away as she recalled the Bridal Veil Falls cascading over a deep terraced silica formation. In some strange way the colours changed from glistening white to a rich red, and later from a subtle yellow to emerald green.

His voice came to her ears. 'Have you been there recently?'

'No.' She stared at the table while thinking of the last time she had stood at the Falls. It had been seven years ago and in the company of this same man—only then he had not been the same man. He had been different, and much too serious to catch, much less to hold, the interest of a seventeen-year-old girl.

Nor, at that time, had he been endowed with the charisma of this man—the aura of male vitality that seemed to ooze from every pore. From where had he acquired these attributes? she wondered. Had success enabled him to develop into a man guaranteed to turn the heads of almost every woman?

The dark eyes took on their piercing glint as he persisted with his questions. 'With whom did you visit the Falls, Sylvia? *Do you even remember?*'

A dull flush rose to her cheeks. 'Of course I remember,' she snapped, determined to keep her own flag flying. 'I also remember I was only seventeen at the time—and fresh out of the confines of boarding school, which was almost akin to coming out of prison. I was looking for a little fun and laughter, with fun-loving friends.'

'And this man you were with?' Lucas queried silkily.

'He was too serious for me. He couldn't understand that I was too young, too immature for the commitment he expected to—to drag from me.'

'Ah, so you do remember it was a proposal of marriage?'

'Of course I remember—and I also remember he'd walked me to the Bridal Veil Falls to offer it.'

'A most appropriate place, by the sound of it. They're aptly named.'

Her voice became tense. 'I couldn't convince him that I wasn't ready for marriage, that I had no intention of stepping out of one cage and into another.' She became exasperated. 'Why do you persist in pretending you've forgotten?'

His voice became hard. 'What makes you think I've remembered?'

'Because you gave yourself away by suggesting I was there with a man, and you know perfectly well that *you were that man*!'

'Let me assure you I've wiped the memory of that affair from my mind, although I do recall the incident of a stinging blow on the ear from a small fist.'

'You had no right to force kisses upon me.'

He ignored the accusation. Instead he gritted at her, 'I offered you everything I had. You retaliated with what's known as a definite brush-off. Since then I've been successful in putting you completely out of my mind—at least, I had been successful until today when you walked into my office.'

'You had no idea I was being sent by the employment agency?'

'Not the slightest. Why did you accept the position?'

'Because I needed the job, of course. What other reason could there be?'

'Well, I just wondered if you had ideas——'

Sylvia was puzzled. 'Ideas of what?'

'Of having another look at the situation—between us.'

Her eyes sparked with anger as she glared at him, her voice becoming icy. 'Are you saying you wondered if I hoped to renew my—my association with you?'

'I'll admit the thought did occur to me. Can't you understand it was a shock to see you after all these years, especially now that——'

'Now that you're successful?' she cut in scathingly. 'That's it, isn't it? You think your success has brought me running back to you. Well, let me tell you, you're mistaken. You were always too serious for me, and I can't see that you're any different now.'

Lucas frowned. 'Serious? Yes, I suppose I was somewhat morbid at that stage. It was a time when life had become mighty serious for me.'

'Oh?' Despite her previous anger Sylvia was interested.

'Only a few months previously I'd lost both my parents. It had knocked the stuffing out of me.'

'I'm sorry—I didn't know. I don't recall that you told me about it.'

'That's because I was unable to speak of it without breaking down like a child. They were killed in a car accident on the highway south of Auckland. Our home was sold and I came to Rotorua to live with my grandfather.'

'At least I can now realise why you were such a—a sombre person.'

'I don't want to sound sorry for myself—but when I met you I was still in a state of shock.'

'I understand,' Sylvia said softly.

'I doubt it.'

'You're forgetting that since then I've lost my own father, so I *do* understand—a little.'

'You didn't lose your mother as well, and your home. You weren't thrown in with an irascible grandfather who'd lost his only son. I can tell you, things were grim.'

She remained silent, not knowing what to say.

Lucas went on, 'And then you appeared on my horizon. You were like a breath of fresh air in a dank environment, a ray of light in a dark room. I reached out, searching for love.'

She was still unable to find words.

'Later, when I began to think more clearly, I realised I didn't know you very well—and that I'd been utterly stupid to ask you to marry me.' The last statement came flatly.

Her chin rose. 'Thank you very much!' she flared, irritated by the words. 'What you're really saying is that you didn't love me at all. You were merely seeking comfort and sympathy.'

'Not at all. In actual fact, I was head over heels.'

'I doubt it. Personally I consider that wounded pride was your main problem.' She pursued relentlessly, 'You've long since become resigned to the loss of your parents, but you've *never* got over the memory of being rejected. It's something your male ego has been unable to tolerate, and my unexpected appearance has stirred it all up again.'

'You're mistaken. Didn't I say I'd put the incident out of my mind?' His jaw tightened as he snapped the words.

She laughed. 'Be honest! You've put *me* out of your mind, but not the fact of having been rejected. For seven years it's been lying dormant, but today my arrival stirred it to life.'

It became his turn to remain silent.

'Why didn't you tell me to get the hell out of it?' she asked. 'Never darken your office door again, and so forth.'

'Because there's work to be done. Clients' taxes to be assessed and paid to the Inland Revenue by a certain date.'

For a moment she toyed with the idea of telling him to find somebody else to do the work, and then she realised that to do so would be unwise. She needed the job, and to throw it back in his face would do nothing to enhance further prospects with the employment agency whose assistance she could need again.

Besides, there was something else that made her hesitate, something she was unable to define. And while she appreciated that being employed by the successful Lucas Carville endowed her with an added dignity, she also knew there was a deeper reason urging her to hold on to the job.

At last she said, 'Well, let's face it. You're in a fix without Miss Ransom, and I need the job. So shall we get back to work? This has been a mighty long lunch hour.'

CHAPTER TWO

DESPITE Sylvia's words, Lucas did not appear to be in a hurry to move. Instead he continued to regard her from across the table.

She became impatient. 'Are you considering contacting the agency again? Perhaps you're having thoughts of replacing me?'

'No. I'd be unwise to throw out someone as efficient as yourself because of what happened seven years ago—especially with so much work piled up on the desk.'

She could only hope the flood of inner relief did not show on her face, and to make sure of this she kept her eyes lowered.

His voice came coldly. 'However, there's just one point I must make clear—in fact, must insist upon. What's past is past, and I've no intention of allowing it to develop again.'

'Develop? I don't understand.'

'I'm referring to my own emotional state of those days.'

'You mean—concerning me?'

'Exactly. At that time I was little more than a callow youth whose nose had been kept at his studies.'

'*Callow youth?* Huh! Are you forgetting you were twenty-three?'

'Nevertheless I knew next to nothing about women, and their wiles, but now I've learnt to enjoy their company when it suits me.'

'But with no intention of being caught,' Sylvia added for him.

Lucas looked at her unsmilingly. 'That's right. I'm glad you can see the situation so clearly.' He rose to his feet. 'Shall we go?'

She stood up and faced him. 'And I'm glad we've had this talk. It's good to know exactly where one stands.'

Little was said as the miles towards Rotorua disappeared, the silences between them being caused by his apparent involvement with his own thoughts. At times she noticed a frown appear on his brow, and on one occasion she made an attempt to probe its reason.

Hesitantly she asked, 'Something about me still bothers you?'

He sent her a side glance. 'Yes, but no doubt it'll pass. It's all a matter of mental control.'

'You're still dwelling on the old days when you took me out a few times?' she queried in an innocent tone.

Tight-lipped, Lucas ignored the question.

She sent him a peep of enquiry, but as no further information appeared to be forthcoming she said, 'Well, thank you for taking me to lunch. It was very pleasant.'

'Only part of the time, I think.'

A smile touched her lips. 'Let's say most of the time, because the air has now been cleared.'

After that her spirits rose and she felt more relaxed, perhaps because she imagined she knew this present-day, this more mature Lucas Carville better than the one he'd termed to be little more than a callow youth. Or was it because she enjoyed sitting beside him while the white Alfa Romeo purred along the highway?

In the restaurant she had found difficulty in keeping her eyes from his handsome features, but now she was able to steal quick peeps at his profile with its straight nose, and at the corner of his rather sensuous lips. She liked the crease which lay below one cheek, almost becoming an elongated dimple when he offered a rare smile.

Nor did the strong, well-shaped hands resting on the wheel escape her attention, and again June's words slipped into her mind. Mr Fantastic, she'd called him. Mr Fantastic indeed—but he had no need to fear any repercussions from their earlier association. In this case, history would not repeat itself because she would not allow her thoughts to revolve around him. There was no chance that he'd go to her head, she assured herself with a surge of determination.

And hadn't he told her in no uncertain terms that their former affair was as dead as the extinct moas that had once roamed the New Zealand bush? Not that it had ever developed into a real affair, but what there had been of it was like those giant birds and *not to be resurrected*.

When they returned to the office Sylvia made haste to settle herself before the computer, where she endeavoured to make up for lost time. Nor did she dally over the afternoon break where interest was betrayed by Karen, whose brown eyes held a mischievous gleam as she probed quite openly.

'That was a nice long lunch hour. We were beginning to wonder if you'd both taken off for foreign parts.'

'Yes, it was,' Sylvia agreed without offering further information. The two were obviously bursting with curiosity.

June put in, 'The Ransom phoned. She sounded very husky—in fact she could hardly speak. She was anxious about the work.'

Sylvia knew the grin on June's face indicated more to come. She sipped her tea in silence, waiting.

June said, 'I told her you'd been sent by the agency, so she asked to speak to you. I had to tell her you were still at lunch. She couldn't believe it because it was after two o'clock.'

Karen took over the story. 'The Ransom then asked to speak to the boss—and June had to tell her he'd taken you to lunch.' She giggled. 'I'd say it's guaranteed to give her recovery the hurry-up!'

Sylvia became thoughtful as she looked from one to the other. She knew they were longing to know where she'd been taken for lunch and why the hour had stretched to such a length, so she came to a decision which made her say, 'If she rings again you may tell her that the boss and I knew each other years ago, and that he merely wanted to catch up on a few things.'

June's eyes widened as she breathed in little more than a whisper, 'Cor, don't tell us you're the one who turned him sour!'

Sylvia was startled. *'Sour?'* she echoed.

'She means he's so serious and—and not easy to approach,' Karen explained.

'I recall he was always rather serious,' said Sylvia.

'The Ransom heard from somewhere that years ago he was nutty about a girl who turned him down.'

'Oh?' Sylvia found difficulty in looking at Karen. She groped for words but could find little to say apart from asking, 'Did you ever hear—anything about her?'

Karen shrugged. 'Nothing, except that she was a blonde. That's why I said that some men are suckers for blondes.' She continued to eye Sylvia's hair thoughtfully.

Sylvia had a sudden urge to leave them, but knew that to do so too hastily could make her appear guilty. It would give them something to ponder about, if they weren't already doing so, so she finished her tea, put her cup down and said casually, 'I'd better get back to the computer.'

She left the staff-room before further questions could arise. So Lucas had been soured? And she had done this to him? Nonsense. He could not have been so deeply affected by her refusal to marry him. Nor did she believe he had avoided the company of other women during the last seven years. He must have taken numerous women to various entertainments—nor would the evening end with a brief goodnight.

Soured was just another of eighteen-year-old June's exaggerations. When that lass had gathered a few more years she'd realise that men of Lucas Carville's calibre did not deny themselves female company for too long. They had needs that could be supplied only by the opposite sex, and in this respect Lucas was no different from any other virile male whose sexuality had been stirred.

Sylvia found herself gazing sightlessly at the computer screen while these thoughts ran through her mind, then she pushed them away and turned to the stack of papers beside her. Just forget his women friends and attend to his clients, she told herself. And there were plenty of the latter whose taxes needed to be assessed.

The amount of work caused the days to slip by rapidly, and during the week she saw very little of Lucas. On one occasion a query took her into his office, where she found him speaking on the phone. She turned to retreat, but his gesture indicated that he wanted her to wait.

Speaking into the receiver, he said, 'It's OK, Maureen, there's no need for you to be so concerned. The job is being done with the utmost competence—yes, she's very good indeed.'

There was a longer pause while he listened before cutting in with a hint of impatience. 'Maureen, will you please understand you are not to return to this office until you're thoroughly well. The 'flu going round appears to be a particularly virulent type, and there's no need to sprinkle its germs over the rest of the staff. Even Amy looked seedy this morning. I hope she's not going down with it.'

Amy? Who's Amy? Sylvia wondered. His housekeeper, perhaps?

Lucas's voice became crisp. 'I can assure you that Sylvia has the work well under control, so you will take another week off. Naturally, your salary will continue as if you were here.' He replaced the receiver and turned to Sylvia. 'Yes—? You have a problem?' His tone was still abrupt.

'Just a small point I'd like to have cleared.'

He moved closer to examine the paper she held, and then a few brief words answered her query. She felt tense as his fingers brushed her hand, but he stepped away almost immediately, turning to other work on his desk, and she felt herself to have been dismissed. Nevertheless, she returned to the computer with his words to Maureen still in her mind—words that indicated that her work was satisfactory.

The rest of the week passed without incident until eleven-thirty on Friday morning when June came into her room. 'There's a man at the desk asking to see you,' the younger girl whispered, her green eyes widening.

Sylvia was surprised. 'Oh? What sort of man?'

'Well, he's tall and fair-haired. Light blue eyes——'

Sylvia sighed. The description sounded like Brian Brookes. What on earth could he want? She went out to the desk, to find herself faced by the man her father had taken into partnership.

The sight of her brought a wide grin to his face. 'Ah, there you are,' he declared breezily. 'Will twelve o'clock be OK?'

She stared at him blankly. 'OK for what?'

'For lunch, of course. I'll pick you up at noon.'

'I've made no arrangement to have lunch with you, Brian.'

'Does that matter? I'll be here to collect you at twelve.'

'You won't, you know,' she said firmly.

He frowned. 'Why not?'

She had no intention of lunching with Brian and she made a spur-of-the-moment decision. 'Because I'll be working through most of my lunch hour apart from having a sandwich in the staff-room.'

'Come now, you can't be as busy as you're making out to be.' His voice had become ironical while he put an arm about her shoulders.

Sylvia shook it off angrily. 'I am definitely very busy.'

His tone became sarcastic. 'Your new boss is something of a slavedriver? Well, another day, perhaps.'

She noticed he did not appear to be unduly crestfallen by her refusal to lunch with him, then she caught her breath as a small cough behind them indicated Lucas's presence. The two men nodded briefly to each other, and as Brian left the office Lucas spoke in a dry tone. 'He's still around, I see.'

Sylvia felt annoyed by the warmth that had risen to her cheeks. 'Yes, he's still living in Rotorua.'

'That's not exactly what I meant.' Lucas's voice had become sardonic as he regarded her heightened colour.

She turned to stare at him. 'Really? Then what did you mean exactly?'

His jaw tightened. 'I think you know the answer to that question without any further explanation from me.'

She continued to stare at him as the answer leapt into her mind. Seven years ago Brian had begun working with her father, his arrival being within a short time of when she had met Lucas. And while Lucas had been lacking in laughter, Brian's spirit of fun had been just what she had been seeking at that time.

Nor had he tried to pin her down to a commitment she was not ready to make. At least, not then. That had come later when she had learnt to know him better and realised he was not the man she wanted to marry. And, as Lucas had now pointed out, he was still around.

The weekend came as a welcome respite from the concentration demanded by the computer. However, it was not a time of complete freedom because it held its own particular chores. Apart from washing her hair and rinsing out a few clothes, Sylvia took over the duties of Wiki, who had both Saturday and Sunday off.

Nor were they arduous tasks, because Ruth Sinclair insisted upon attending to her patients' more personal needs herself. Nevertheless, to Sylvia it was like living in two different worlds. In the one at the office she learnt to appreciate her own ability and skills, while the one at home taught her to appreciate her youth and good health.

'Always be kind to elderly people,' her mother had preached when Sylvia had been little more than a child. 'Some day you yourself will be old.'

And then the time had come when Sylvia had reminded her of those words by saying, 'That thought really started you off with this place. It's like a ship that's come home to port.'

'At least it's saving my reason,' Ruth had pointed out seriously.

She was an attractive woman who had never lost her slim figure. Although she was not yet fifty her husband's death had streaked her blonde hair with threads of silver, and had taken a little of the sparkle from her blue eyes. However, it had done nothing to dampen her energy.

'I must do something to stop myself from waiting for him to walk in the door—something to combat grief,' she had said a short time after their bereavement. 'I can't sit about thinking only of myself and moaning about my loss. I must think of others.'

Sylvia had nodded. She knew the feeling of waiting for her father to walk in the door.

And then an incident occurred which altered the scene. At the time it had seemed to be trivial enough, but it pointed the way towards solving Ruth's problem.

It concerned their next-door neighbours, who had arranged to attend a wedding in Hamilton. The city lay seventy miles away, and they had intended to stay there for the weekend.

But when Ruth spoke to her friend across the fence she thought the latter appeared to be slightly downcast. 'Aren't you going to Hamilton today?' she had asked.

The neighbour had shaken her head. 'I'm afraid not. I suppose you know George's mother has come to live with us. She's no trouble and we're very fond of her, but at the moment she's not very well. We feel we're unable to leave her alone in the house, so——'

'So she's clipped your wings where this weekend jaunt to Hamilton is concerned,' Ruth had finished for her. She had thought quickly and had then said, 'There's no need for her to do so. There are five bedrooms in this old house, three of them just crying out to be used. Take me to meet her and I'll invite her to spend the weekend in one of them.'

And that had been the beginning. Within a short time the empty bedrooms in the rambling single-storeyed house had found occupants, and even if it had begun with a simple case of granny-sitting, Ruth's nursing experience had soon enabled her to take in people who lived alone but who required care during a period of convalescence after an illness.

And now, as Sylvia carried tea and pikelets to an elderly man who enjoyed the morning sun in a sheltered corner of the veranda, she realised how successful the project had become. She spoke to him brightly, 'Morning tea, Mr Mackenzie.'

He put down his newspaper and peered at the small tray, then spoke with a soft Scottish accent. 'Aye, thank you—your mother's a fine hand at the pikelets. My, but she's a bonny lass! If I could drop thirty years from these old shoulders she wouldn't stay a widdy woman for long.'

Sylvia smiled but said nothing. Nor was there any need to tell him that she had made the pikelets, as they were one of her Saturday morning tasks.

He went on. 'There's just one wee thing wrong with this place—aye, there is that.'

Sylvia sent him a startled look. 'Oh? What do you mean?'

He chuckled. 'It's so hard to leave.'

Relieved, she laughed. 'Ah, but you'll be compensated by feeling in better health.'

'Aye, I will that.' He hesitated, then asked, 'When is that Mrs Sykes in Room One leaving?'

Sylvia frowned. 'Mrs Sykes? I believe relatives are taking her to Hamilton tomorrow. Does she worry you?'

His eyes twinkled. 'I'm wondering if she fancies me. Won't leave me alone. Drat the woman, she's coming now with her constant chatter about the important people she knows. She's nothing but a name-dropper!'

Sylvia turned to see a large woman walking slowly along the veranda towards them.

As she approached Jock Mackenzie said gruffly, 'You'll excuse my hips not allowing me to spring to my feet, Mrs Sykes.'

The woman ignored the remark as she turned to Sylvia. 'Ah, tea and pikelets—I'll have mine here with Mr Mackenzie.'

'Yes, of course.' Sylvia sent a hasty glance at the scowl on the old man's face, then hurried towards the kitchen. With Ruth she had long since learnt that some patients were more affable than others.

When she returned to the veranda Mrs Sykes was holding forth about her cousin, dear Lady Ursula, who would be coming to fetch her tomorrow. 'Of course Lady Ursula has *servants*,' she informed the old man. 'And as you know, *real* servants are a thing of the past in this country.'

Sylvia was forced to suppress a giggle as she regarded Jock. His head down, he was dozing, and she realised that this was his way of telling Mrs Sykes she had become a bore.

On returning to the kitchen, she spoke to her mother. 'Mrs Sykes is really leaving tomorrow?'

'Yes. I understand she'll be surrounded by people who'll rush to her beck and call.'

'How very nice for her!'

'We'll attend to her room the moment she's left.'

'You won't leave it for Wiki to do on Monday?'

'Certainly not. It's my number one room and when empty must be kept in readiness at all times.' Ruth changed the subject by saying, 'I notice you've said very little about your new job. Do you feel you'll be happy in it?'

'Yes, I think it will be all right,' Sylvia admitted evasively.

'This Lucas Carville—is he the one you knew years ago?'

'The same.' There was no need to go into details, she decided.

'I recall he was a serious young man,' said Ruth.

'I doubt that he's changed very much,' Sylvia replied, knowing that she herself was the one who had changed. And instead of considering Lucas to be over-serious, she now looked on him as one who had stability. He was, in fact, a man of substance.

When Sylvia woke on Monday morning she was conscious of a strange feeling of excitement. Deep down she knew its cause lay in the expectancy of contact with Lucas, but in this she was to be faced by anticlimax, because she saw little of him.

Her second week at the office proved to be as busy as the first, but apart from a few brief moments each morning when he came into her room to leave papers on her desk, the expected contact barely existed. In fact, all she was able to hold on to was the tang of his after-shave which assailed her senses until her mind became lost in the complexities of income tax figures.

It was not that she *wanted* him to spend more time than necessary in her room, she assured herself firmly. Nor did she expect him to pay her special attention. He was much too busy to do so—the work piling beside her being mute evidence of that fact.

Besides, could she honestly say she deserved any special attention from Lucas Carville? A glimpse into the past brought an echoing answer of no—*definitely no*. Further, she had only to recall the terse words he'd flung at her during that lunch hour at Waiotapu. What's past is past, he'd said in a cold hard voice.

And so the week passed uneventfully, until Friday afternoon when she took completed work into his office and was surprised by the sight of flowers on his desk. The papers she carried almost slid from her fingers as she gazed at the large cellophane-covered basket of pink, white and yellow carnations. They had been arranged with florist expertise and adorned by a cluster of pink satin-like ribbon, while the card attached to them appeared to be of the more expensive variety.

At the time of her entry he was speaking on the phone. 'Right, Maureen, we'll be glad to see you back on Monday.' There was a pause while he listened, then a smile broke over his face as he said, 'You may look forward to a surprise.'

Sylvia's eyes examined the flowers. Surprise? Were they intended as a surprise for Maureen?

As he replaced the receiver she said carefully, 'They're lovely.'

'Yes, she loves flowers.'

'They're for Maureen?'

A smile of amusement crossed his face. 'What makes you think so?'

'You spoke of a surprise for her and I—I just assumed. Not that it concerns me, of course.'

'The surprise I referred to concerns you. I was speaking of your ability, which has also surprised me.'

'Oh.' A flush of pleasure rose to Sylvia's cheeks. 'I'm glad you're happy with my work.' *Glad?* It was an understatement.

'As for the flowers, read the card.' The order was snapped in an abrupt tone.

She hesitated. 'Really, I've no wish to pry. You may send flowers to whom you wish.'

'Read the card,' he said again, this time with less irritation tinging the words.

Obeying reluctantly, yet conscious of curiosity, Sylvia opened the card and read, *To dear Amy, wishing her a happy birthday and many more of them to follow. Love from Lucas.* She raised her eyes to his, then found herself unable to resist the question. 'Who is Amy?'

'She's Mrs Grayson, my mother's widowed sister—which makes her my aunt. She lives with me.'

'I didn't know you have an aunt living with you.'

'That's not surprising. After all, there's so little you do know about me.' His tone had become full of mockery, then it softened as he went on, 'After her husband's death Grandfather invited her to live with us.'

'That was kind of him.'

'He was being more cunning than philanthropic. He wanted another woman in the house—someone to act as a companion for his very good housekeeper.'

'It was successful?'

'Very—because Amy is a sweet person. However, when the housekeeper left to live with her daughter in the South Island Aunt stayed on in her place. Unfortunately she hasn't been well during the last week. A touch of this wretched 'flu, I think.'

Sylvia kept the reprimand from her voice. 'Aren't you a little late in taking flowers to her? The birthday is almost over.'

'I'll admit I forgot about it. Even now she'll be lucky to see them before morning because I have an appointment that'll keep me late. In fact it's in a short time,' Lucas added with a swift glance at his watch.

Sylvia felt a sudden sympathy for his aunt. She looked at the flowers, which would need additional water, then offered impulsively. 'Would you like me to deliver them for you? It's nearly closing time and it would be no trouble to do so.'

His face brightened. 'By Jove, that would be a help. If you'd do so it would lighten a dull evening for her, and I'd be most grateful. You drive out of the city and up the hill to where the houses overlook the lake.'

A most expensive area, she thought, watching him sketch a road map.

'There, it's on that point—you can't miss it. I'll phone and tell her you're coming.' He lifted the receiver and pressed buttons.

The person at the other end answered immediately, indicating that she was right beside the phone.

Lucas said, 'Amy—? Happy Birthday. I forgot to say it this morning. Yes, I know I'm busy, but I should have remembered.' There was a pause while he listened, then said, 'No, I shan't be home soon. I have a meeting and I'll be late, I'm afraid. In the meantime I'm sending one of my girls with a little something for you.'

One of his girls. The phrase irritated Sylvia, reminding her that she was *staff* and that it was unlikely she'd ever be anything else. Nor was she being *sent*, she thought crossly. She had offered to take the flowers. She became aware he was frowning.

'You're in bed? Amy, you assured me you were over the worst of that nasty cold. Very well, I'll tell her to walk in the front door and go straight upstairs. I'll give her my key.'

A short time later Sylvia drove along a road that wound round the lakeside hills. Nor had she any difficulty in finding the white-timbered house with its orange-tiled roof, its neat garden and shaven lawns. And as she studied its situation on a point which gave most of the windows views of the lake, she decided it was like its owner. It had stability.

A path bordered by bright clumps of polyanthus led to the front door, and, holding the basket of carnations carefully, she inserted the key. The action gave her a strange feeling of familiarity with Lucas, but she brushed it aside knowing that *that* opportunity had been lost seven years ago.

The panelled hall was square in shape, its thick red and blue carpet continuing up the stairs which turned halfway before reaching the landing. Sylvia ascended them, then looked for the third door on the left as directed by Lucas.

A voice answered her knock. 'Come in.'

The woman in the bed appeared to be about sixty. She was small, grey-haired, and as her hazel eyes rested upon the carnations she said huskily, 'Aren't they just beautiful? Thank you so much for bringing them to me.' She looked at Sylvia. 'You must be new in the office. I haven't seen you before—' The words ended in a slight fit of coughing. As it subsided she said, 'Don't come too near, I've got this horrible cold.'

Sylvia said, 'I started a fortnight ago. I'm Sylvia Sinclair.'

'Oh, well, that's why I haven't seen you. I've been poorly for about that time.'

'Is there anything I can do for you?'

Amy Grayson shook her head. 'No, thank you. I've become accustomed to struggling for myself.'

'You shouldn't be alone in the house when you're not well.'

'I don't like to be a nuisance—although I must admit it gets lonely at times—' Her words were cut by a spasm of coughing which brought an expression of pain to her face.

It did not escape Sylvia. 'Something hurts?' she asked.

Amy nodded. 'Yes—it's under my ribs, at my back.'

'You've told Lucas?'

The grey head was shaken gently. 'No. I've no wish to worry him. He'd insist on the doctor and then the man wouldn't be able to get into the house, because I like the doors to be locked when I'm in bed. She coughed again, this time with difficulty.

Sylvia became practical. 'Has your temperature been taken?'

'No. I doubt there's a thermometer in the house. Lucas is so healthy, and I'm not usually in this stupid state.'

Sylvia placed a hand on the older woman's forehead. Her eyes narrowed as she felt its heat, then she said, 'I think you're rather warm—and you look flushed. I believe you need proper care and attention. Nor should you be getting in and out of bed to find something to eat.'

'Eat? I can assure you that food is the last thing I want—although I'll admit to being thirsty.'

Sylvia looked at her thoughtfully. 'How would you like a spell with somebody to care for you?'

A tear trickled down Amy's cheek. 'It would be heavenly. I must say I get very depressed, Do you know of somebody who'd come to me?'

'No. I'd take you to somebody. May I use your phone? I guessed there was one beside the bed.'

A quick call to her mother rapidly settled the situation which resulted in Amy's small figure being wrapped warmly, then assisted downstairs to the garage which was attached to the house. Sylvia drove her car into the garage and within minutes Amy was being whisked to Sophia Street, where she was installed in the number one bedroom. Ruth took one look at her and phoned the doctor.

Sylvia found herself assailed by a tense nervousness as she awaited Lucas's reaction. A note had been left for him on the kitchen table, and beside it she had put his key. He'd see them as he walked in from the adjoining garage, but now she began to fear he would decide she'd been high-handed in moving his aunt to her mother's home.

She did not consider him to be an uncaring person where his aunt was concerned. The carnations, which had been brought with them, were proof enough of that. It was just that his mind had been taken up with so many business matters and clients' tax problems.

Nor had his aunt admitted to the seriousness of her condition. So, unless she'd told him, how could he possibly know that it hurt her to cough?

As the thoughts ran through her mind she began to shift the blame from Lucas to Amy Grayson, whose reluctance to worry him had kept her silent. And in the meantime she herself would just have to await the wrath to come.

It arrived next morning when she saw the white Alfa Romeo sweep into the drive. She watched through the window as he strode up the veranda steps to the front door, and on opening it to him she forced a smile and said, 'I see you found my note.'

Tight-lipped, his tone was grim. 'I certainly did!'

She led him to the number one bedroom where she said, 'I'll be in the garden if you want me. I have to do the flowers.' She went outside, where she picked daffodils, anemones and blue grape hyacinths almost without seeing them.

Nor had she long to wait before Lucas came striding across the lawn towards her, and for several moments she said nothing, waiting for his anger to descend because she'd moved his aunt without his consent. However, the outburst did not come—or perhaps he had himself under control. Nevertheless she sensed a coolness in his attitude, then was surprised to realise that his anger seemed to be directed towards himself.

His jaw tight, he said, 'Amy tells me your mother rang the doctor the moment you brought her here.'

'Yes. Mother has a medical friend who usually answers her call as soon as possible.'

'She appears to have a touch of pleurisy.'

'A very firm touch, I think.'

Irritated, he rasped, 'If she'd told me she had pains round her ribs I'd have had her into a private hospital right smartly!'

Sylvia's tone became cool. 'I think you'll find she's in good hands.' Then, reproachfully, 'Even my untrained eye could see she was running a temperature.'

'I'll not make excuses by saying I've been busy. You'll have seen that for yourself.'

She nodded as she said, 'Come into the kitchen. It's time for me to make the pikelets.'

Lucas followed her, then settled himself on a window seat while she arranged the flowers in vases. They were removed from the kitchen, and his scrutiny became more intense as she measured the ingredients for the pikelets.

He said nothing while she counted six rounded tablespoons of flour and three of caster sugar into a sieve, then added a pinch of salt. But when she carefully flattened a teaspoon each of baking soda and cream of tartar he asked, 'Are you always so meticulous in everything you do?'

She spoke drily. 'Two weeks of my work should enable you to judge for yourself. Are you satisfied or dissatisfied?'

'More than satisfied,' he admitted gravely.

'Thank you for the high praise.' Her fingers shook slightly as she picked up a fresh egg which she broke into the sifted dry ingredients before stirring gently with a fork. It was followed by a scant cup of creamy milk which also received a gentle blending with a fork.

He left the window seat and came to peer into the bowl. 'Does my presence disturb you?' The question came casually.

It did, but she had been hoping it didn't show. 'Not at all,' she lied, then managed to ask casually, 'Why do you ask?'

'You seem to be hesitant over the mixing of those pikelets. What's more, you have a lumpy mixture. Shouldn't it be smooth?'

'No. It's supposed to be stirred as little as possible and left as a lumpy mixture,' she explained. 'Now I'll let it stand until the electric frying pan is the right heat.'

He continued to watch while small dabs of mixture slid from a dessertspoon to the pan's greased surface. Within a short time they bubbled and were turned to brown on the other side, then, when the second batch was ready to turn, he took the spatula from her hand.

'Let me do it. I'm sure I'd be good at turning pikelets.'

'Don't you dare flop one on top of the other,' Sylvia warned, turning to put out cups and saucers for morning tea.

And then a man's voice spoke from behind them. 'What's this—a new cook in the kitchen?'

They turned to see Brian standing in the doorway, his expression belligerent as his eyes rested on Lucas.

He went on, 'Am I being deceived, or do I see the high and mighty Lucas Carville, builder of a castle, engaged in menial work?' His jocular tone did nothing to conceal the sneer hovering about his lips.

CHAPTER THREE

SYLVIA was puzzled by Brian's remark. *Castle?* What was he talking about? However, she decided to ignore it as she said, 'Have you come to see Mother? She's on the side veranda with Mr Mackenzie.'

He gave a short laugh. 'No, I have not come to see your mother. As it happens, I've come to see you. I've decided it's time we talked again—about you know what.'

More than aware of his meaning, she prevaricated, 'I can't think of anything.'

Brian grinned. 'Then I'll have to refresh your memory. This afternoon I need to photograph a house in Tarawera Road, and after that we'll take a drive past the Blue and Green lakes to the Buried Village. I'll call for you at two o'clock.'

'You won't, you know.' The drawled words came from Lucas, who did not even bother to look at Brian as he spoke.

Brian frowned, then demanded, 'Why not?'

'Because she doesn't require heavy discussion of any sort. She's been toiling all the week and an afternoon of relaxation is called for—which I intend to provide.' Lucas paused to turn the pikelets before adding, 'Strangely, I had the same destination in mind.'

'We'll see about that!' snarled Brian. 'You'd better know that Sylvia and I have an understanding——'

Sylvia cut in impatiently, 'Don't be stupid, Brian. I've told you often enough—I just can't get it through to you.'

His tone became appealing. 'You know it was your father's dearest wish,' he reminded her.

'Only if it also happened to be my dearest wish—which it isn't. Daddy would never try to force me into—anything.'

Brian glared at Lucas, his light blue eyes alive with suppressed fury. 'I suppose this is your doing. You've turned her head!'

Lucas shrugged but said nothing. Instead he spooned more dabs of mixture into the pan.

Brian gritted at Sylvia, 'Don't imagine you'll get far with *him*! He's known as being one who's not too fond of women.'

Lucas replaced the bowl on the table with a bang. He swung round to face Brian, his eyes narrowed, his jaw tight. 'What the hell do you mean by that remark?'

Brian shrugged. 'I know only what I've been told—and on very good authority.'

'Whose authority? Explain yourself, or I'll belt the living daylights out of you!' Lucas took several steps towards the other man.

Brian backed away. 'Hey, steady on, don't get rough! It was simply that this—this person said you seldom take a girl out and that your aunt is forced to live like a recluse.'

Sylvia found herself defending Lucas. 'You're being ridiculous, Brian. How can you possibly know what Lucas does, or how his aunt lives?'

Brian looked smug. 'I've heard the odd bit about him.'

'From whom?' she persisted.

'Surely you wouldn't expect me to mention a name?'

'A name? So all this rubbish has come from one person?' Sylvia queried scornfully.

'I doubt that it's rubbish,' Brian retorted. 'This person knows him well enough to realise he's worked his guts out to build a castle.'

Sylvia looked at him wordlessly. There it was again—the reference to a castle. What did he mean?

Brian went on scathingly, 'And now that he's reached the top he's sitting in his tower like a king. The only trouble is that he refuses to allow anyone to share it with him. So you can see she knows him very well indeed.'

'She?' Lucas stared at him. 'Well, that certainly narrows the field. '*She*, you say,' he mused.

Brian gave a snort of derision. 'I must say it's amusing to watch the king of the castle making *pikelets*!' And with that parting sneer he left.

There was silence after his departure. Sylvia, who had returned to the frying pan during the argument, took a quick peep at Lucas, who stood with his legs apart, his hands deep in his pockets and a scowl on his face. And while she longed to enquire into the question of the castle, instinct warned that this was not the moment to do so.

Besides, she herself had her own reason for displeasure, and as she put the buttered pikelets on a plate she said, 'I have no recollection of making arrangements to go out this afternoon.'

'It was a spur-of-the-moment decision. The fact that Brookes declared he had need to talk to you reminded me that I also have a few words to say.'

'Then speak up.' Here it comes, she thought. *Reprimand*.

But he said, 'It can wait until this afternoon. Morning tea has already been delayed, I think.'

His high-handed certainty that she would accompany him niggled her into a state of irritation, and for several moments she considered a refusal. But even as she sought for words she became aware that her reluctance lacked depth, and that she really did want to go with him.

Nevertheless she began, 'I really have things to do. The weekend is my only free time—'

'Then it should at least hold a short period of relaxation, like looking at the Blue and Green lakes. Agreed?'

She ignored the last question by saying, 'This is your aunt's tray. Would you like to take it to her? You can tell her you made the pikelets.'

He chuckled. 'She'd never believe me!'

At that moment Ruth came into the kitchen. To Sylvia she said, 'Jock Mackenzie is becoming impatient for his morning tea.' Then she examined the tray Lucas carried. 'You're taking that to your aunt? She must have an antibiotic as well. By the way, you'll stay with us for lunch?'

'Thank you.' The answer came gravely.

'Did I hear Brian's voice?' Ruth queried.

Sylvia spoke casually. 'Yes. He just—looked in.'

Nor was his name mentioned again until they drove along Sophia Street and turned into the busy length of Fenton Street, where Lucas turned to her and said, 'You're sure you're relaxing with the right man? I mean, I don't want you to feel bullied into coming with me simply because I'm your boss.'

'No, not at all. I'm ready to enjoy myself.' It was true, and she leaned against the seat feeling happily content.

She had considered her wardrobe carefully and had finally decided that a gold-flecked pleated skirt and matching jacket with a cream blouse had more feminine appeal than a leisure suit of trousers and top. She had taken extra care with her make-up, and as she'd stepped into the Alfa Romeo she had known that Lucas's eyes took in every inch of her appearance.

'You're looking very attractive,' he had murmured in a low voice that held a ring of sincerity.

'Thank you.' His words had caused a glow of contentment which had sent a smile to her lips, and she was still in a cheerful mood as the car left Fenton Street to follow a branching highway that led round the eastern side of Lake Rotorua. Another turn took them beyond the residential area, and after driving for a short distance they stopped in a roadside parking area beside two lakes, one blue and the other quite green.

The two expanses of water lying so close to each other were surrounded by tree-covered hills. At the roadside they were divided by a narrow isthmus of land which provided an excellent vantage point from which to compare the difference in their colours.

It seemed natural for Lucas to take her hand as they climbed the slight rise, then stood to gaze from the length of the Green Lake to the circular shape of the Blue Lake. 'It's amazing!' he exclaimed. 'They're so close together, yet one is quite blue while the other is definitely green. There must be a reason for the difference.'

Sylvia tried to ignore the tingling fire in her hand caused by his touch, and, keeping her voice casual, she said, 'The contrasting colours show well on a fine day, so we're fortunate.' She paused, then reminisced, 'Wiki told me that the long lake reflects the enfolding arms of green hills and trees, while the round lake smiles back at the sky.'

'Perhaps that's the truth of it, unless there are different minerals in the waters. After all, the whole area of Rotorua is one big spa. It's a strange mass of boiling springs, bubbling mud and tiny volcanoes——'

'Not all of them tiny, as the people of Te Wairoa discovered when Tarawera mountain blew its top last century,' she reminded him.

They returned to the car and drove a few miles to a tree-sheltered area that nestled on the edge of Lake Tarawera. Surrounded by hills, it had once been the starting point for visits to a world-famous tourist attraction known as the Pink and White Terraces. However, the Terraces no longer existed, because they had been devastated in 1886 by the horrific eruption of Tarawera which rose like a flat-headed giant across the expanse of smooth water. There had been much loss of life, while Maori villages had been buried beneath eight feet of volcanic mud and debris.

Lucas parked the car, and after paying a small fee they wandered along paths leading between excavated homes, the remains of the two-storeyed tourist hotel, the flourmill and other buildings that had once formed the village of Te Wairoa.

As they paused at a dark hole that looked like the entrance to a cave Sylvia said, 'This is where the witch doctor lived. He was reputed to have been a hundred and ten years of age. The entire disaster was blamed on him because, only a few days previously, he'd predicted it would happen.'

'How could he do that?' Lucas sounded sceptical.

'Apparently there were places where extra thermal activity had popped out of the ground, and the lake was abnormally high. And then there were tales of a phantom canoe on the lake—a large old-time canoe full of warriors with bent heads. It was seen by numerous tourists who were on their way to see the Pink and White Terraces. They declared it came close enough to see the flash of paddles.'

She paused, waiting for him to scoff with derision or to ask what those same tourists had been drinking, but he merely said, 'I've read about it. I believe one man even made a sketch of it.' Then, looking about him, he added, 'The place holds an aura of sadness, almost as though savouring its memories of the past.'

She looked at him quickly. 'You feel it too? To be honest, Te Wairoa always depresses me—except that I like to see the falls.'

They made their way towards the stream and then along its bank to where the water plunged over a cliff before rushing along lower ground towards the lake. A steep path descended near the narrow, precipitous fall, twisting down almost a hundred and thirty feet, and as they made their way to the lower level Lucas took a firm grip on Sylvia's hand.

Again his touch caused her to catch her breath, and once more she almost imagined a glow of warmth creeping up her arm; however, the necessity to watch her steps on the steep incline enabled her to appear nonchalant.

Nor did he release her hand when they reached the lower level, where they paused to gaze up at the single stream that hurtled down beside the rocky wall. Then, as they left it, the haze of dreamy contentment still clung to her as they continued along the path to where trees stretched branches above their heads.

Fantails fluttered about them, almost brushing their shoulders in efforts to snap at small clouds of hovering, tiny insects, and as Sylvia raised her face to follow the flight of one bird Lucas bent swiftly to drop a light kiss on her forehead.

The unexpectedness of it caused her to stand still, then, staring at him, she spoke in even tones. 'That's not allowed. What's past is past and not to be started again. Remember your own words?' She walked along the path ahead of him.

A few strides took him to her side, his hands on her shoulders swinging her round to face him. His eyes held a strange light as they stared down into her own. 'Sylvia—it's a lovely name. I suppose you know it means a wood nymph?' His arms went about her, holding her close to him. 'I've never held a wood nymph before. They're not easy to catch.'

'Catch?' The word rang with indignation. 'Have you the temerity to imagine you've *caught* me?'

'Nevertheless, my wood nymph, you'll not deny me a kiss in a sylvan glade.' His arms tightened about her as his gaze held her own, his expression becoming inscrutable.

Taken by surprise, she let a small gasp escape her, then her heart leapt as Lucas bent his head, his mouth covering hers in a kiss that was gentle until it suddenly deepened to betray a rising passion.

She drew back, staring at him in wide-eyed astonishment. 'Aren't you forgetting the—the dangers of—of an emotional situation?'

'My emotions are well under control,' he informed her in a voice that was surprisingly cool. 'How are your own?'

'Com-completely under control.' She tried to sound haughty.

'That's all right, then.' Again the dark eyes held her own for several long moments before he drew her even closer, and this time there could be no doubting the intensity of the kiss which became teasingly seductive as it urged her lips apart.

The strength of his arms gave her a strange sense of security, and despite her efforts to keep a grip on her common sense Sylvia found herself responding. She trembled as her heart began to thump, causing her pulses to race until a shaft of cold clear thinking pierced her brain. Watch yourself, it warned.

This is nothing more than a whim on his part, it told her. It can lead only to trouble and possible heartache, because he's no longer the Lucas you knew years ago. He's now a successful—in fact a sophisticated man of the world, whose kisses are vastly different from those cool lip-brushes of seven years ago.

Besides, he's your boss. You're merely one of his staff, so for Pete's sake remember it. A few more kisses like these and he'll expect more than your efficiency at the computer. Much more than you're ready to give.

Gently, Sylvia released herself from his arms, and as she did so the sound of approaching voices could be heard. A nervous laugh escaped her as she uttered inanely, 'Saved by the bell!'

But there was no answering amusement in the eyes that stared down at her. Fire still smouldered within their depths and his face remained serious. '*Saved?* You considered yourself to be in danger?'

Instead of replying she turned and hastened along the path. Yes, she was definitely in danger of falling beneath the charm of Lucas Carville, and this was something she had no intention of doing. Nor must he be allowed to guess that he had an effect upon her.

A few strides took him to her side, and as the path rose steeply, twisting and turning beneath trees as it climbed back towards the higher level, he took her arm. She accepted his assistance calmly, but by the time they reached the top she was breathless and her legs were shaking. And again she was aware of his touch.

He led her to the tea-room, where it was a relief to sit down, and as she sipped her tea she stared unseeingly at a display of photographs taken before and after the Tarawera eruption. The walk had also made her feel hungry, and as she bit into a sandwich she sensed that Lucas had lapsed into a serious frame of mind. Was he regretting those kisses on the lower path? Was he searching for words that would tell her he feared she would take too much meaning from their intensity?

She waited while he looked at her in silence, instinct warning that he had a definite statement to make. That was why they were here, wasn't it? In the kitchen he'd said he had something to say to her. Was it about the past? However, when the words came they surprised her. They were not about the past. They were about the here and now.

Frowning, he demanded. 'I want an explanation.'

Her brows rose. 'Oh? About what?'

'Why did you take my aunt to your mother's home?'

'Because she needed care and attention, of course. How can you ask such a question?'

Lucas's eyes narrowed. 'Are you sure that's the only reason?'

She was puzzled. 'What other could there be?'

'I wondered if you had some other—motive in mind.'

'Like what?' She stared at him across the top of her cup.

'Actually I believe you had a couple of motives in mind. One was to discredit me.'

Sylvia felt bewildered. '*Discredit?* I don't understand.'

His jaw tightened. 'I mean you were trying to make it appear as though I'd neglected my aunt, so you took over to drive the point home. You removed her without my permission.'

'She has a will of her own. She didn't have to come with me.'

'I think you were persuasive.'

'And you take a dim view of it?'

'I do. A mighty dim view——'

She cut in, 'Then let me assure you, your view would have been a sight more murky if she'd become really ill. Pneumonia could have set in—nor should she have been alone in the house.'

'She knows she can have a companion any time she likes, but for some silly female reason she refuses to have anyone else messing about in her kitchen. She may be small in body, but she's big in determination.'

'At least you should have called a doctor,' Sylvia insisted.

'Naturally I'd have done so if I'd realised the necessity. I'm now sure she's kept the severity of her cold from me.'

'She admitted she had no wish to worry you,' Sylvia conceded. 'And even I know you're busy.' She thought for a moment, then added, 'But you've probably always been busy building whatever it is that Brian declared you've been constructing. Something about a castle, wasn't it?' she queried casually, hoping he would explain those enigmatic words that had come in such a sarcastic tone from Brian.

Lucas stared at the table before murmuring thoughtfully, 'There are only two people who have ever heard a mention of that particular castle.'

'Oh? Who are they?'

'My aunt—and Maureen. I can discount gossip from Amy, and I thought I could have relied upon Maureen's discretion. However, I understand she's known Brookes for years, so no doubt she's chatted to him.'

Sylvia tried to sound vaguely interested. 'Where is this castle? It sounds very grand.'

He gave a short laugh. 'It's only in my mind. Purely imaginary, you understand.'

'No, I don't understand. You don't impress me as being one who imagines *castles*. Your feet are much more firmly on the ground.'

The lines about his mouth became sardonic. 'Nor, I suppose, can you understand that the first foundation stones were laid by you.'

Sylvia straightened in her chair, staring at him in disbelief. 'You must be joking! What do you mean?'

'I mean that you were the driving force, the real reason behind its beginning,' he told her coolly.

Her eyes widened. 'How could that be possible?'

'You see, I knew you wouldn't understand.'

She became exasperated. 'For heaven's sake, explain yourself!'

He sighed, betraying a hint of weary impatience. 'OK—but please make an effort to understand that what was brushed aside so lightly by yourself was of real importance to me. My hopes had crumbled about me and I became depressed.'

'You mean, after——'

'That's right. After you turned me down. Rejection is the word for throwing a man's love back in his face.'

'You sound thoroughly sorry for yourself,' she snapped, irritated by the way his words niggled at her conscience.

'I was at that time, but not any longer, because those days have long since gone. I've toughened up and am now immune to the wiles of women. Besides——'

'The past is past,' Sylvia finished, flinging the words at him.

'Exactly. However, I'm glad you're still able to recall what must have been a mere incident to you.'

She felt uncomfortable, her cheeks becoming flushed as she said plaintively, 'Why are you attacking me in this manner? If you're set on convincing me I behaved in a ghastly manner you're succeeding admirably. But at least you survived the ordeal.' She drew a deep breath to calm her irritation. 'So where does the castle come in?'

'It was my grandfather's idea. He could see I was in a state of depression—I mean apart from the upset caused by my parents' deaths—and he dragged the reason for it from me.'

'You told him about me?' The words came in a whisper.

'Why not? You were the root of my trouble. He told me I'd been fortunate. A lucky escape, he called it.'

'Did he indeed?' Sylvia's face went scarlet with indignation.

'He pointed out that I was an eligible bachelor and that had you been a mercenary type you could have married me without an atom of love on your part, and that I'd be too besotted to realise it.'

'But I didn't. At least that was something in my favour,' she defended, the words coming coldly.

'He then suggested I cast my mind in a different direction.'

'You mean—away from me.'

'Exactly. Grandfather had a flair for business. He put money at my disposal and said, "There you are, my boy—go build yourself a castle." Metaphorically speaking, of course. He also bet me I'd be unable to double the cash within a certain period.'

'And you did?'

Lucas nodded. 'I just happened to be lucky on the Stock Exchange, and somehow I seemed to go on from there. Eventually the remainder of Grandfather's money came to me, but at least I'd had the satisfaction of knowing I hadn't disappointed him.' He fell silent, his expression softening as he recalled the help his grandfather had given him.

Sylvia said nothing, waiting for him continue, but when he appeared to be lost behind a veil of reminiscence she asked, 'What else did your grandfather say?' then immediately regretted the question.

He sent her a mocking grin. 'He declared there was nothing like a castle to bring a girl to heel.'

It took several moments for the words to register in her mind. When they did the blood rushed to her face, turning her cheeks scarlet, until it slowly drained away to leave her pale with wrath. 'Are you implying that I've—*come to heel*?'

He shrugged. 'You asked what Grandfather had said. I've merely told you. I can't help it if you don't like the answer.'

Suspicions began to grow in her mind—suspicions that made her go cold with anger. Keeping her voice steady, she demanded, 'Is it possible you imagine your castle is the reason I took the job in your office?'

His tone became sardonic. 'You must forgive me if I—er—pondered the question.'

'And your aunt—you said you believed I had a *couple* of motives for putting her in Mother's care. One was to discredit you, but you haven't yet admitted to the other. Surely you can't possibly think I took her home as a—a means of—of assisting myself towards a closer association with—with——'

'The king of the castle?' Lucas suggested. 'Can you blame me for wondering? At least I'm being thoroughly honest.'

Pride came to her rescue. 'Oh yes, I can appreciate that. Then allow me to put your mind at ease. There'll be no further need for you to either ponder or wonder about these questions,' she hissed.

'No? Why would that be?' he drawled.

'Because I'll not be there. I'll leave—and you can have my notice here and now.'

'You'd leave me in the lurch with so much work to be done?'

'Maureen will be back on Monday.'

'She needs assistance, as you can see for yourself.'

'The employment agency will soon replace me.'

'So you'd desert me again?' he jeered softly.

Sylvia was silent, unable to find words or to even look at him, and, feeling bitterly hurt, she realised he had goaded her into giving notice because he wanted her out of his sight.

'You said you took the job because you needed the work,' he reminded her.

'I was not entirely desperate,' she informed him loftily. 'Brian is always——' She stopped, suddenly aware of what she had been about to say.

Lucas became alert. 'Yes? Brian is always—what?'

'Nagging me to go back to the real estate agency,' she confessed in a low tone.

'But you persistently refuse?'

Sylvia nodded wordlessly.

'Why?'

'Because he becomes too—possessive. He imagines that because Daddy left him as a trustee he has the right to—to have a say over my private affairs.'

'To be honest, I thought you'd have been married to him by now.'

Anger flashed into her eyes. 'As you can see, I am not.'

'Wasn't he the laughing cavalier who appeared on your scene soon after my own arrival?'

'That's right,' she flashed at him. 'But he stayed, while you didn't.' She looked away, recalling her shocked dismay when she'd learnt that Brian Brookes had been named as one of the trustees of her father's estate. However, she did not see that this gave him the right to walk in and out of their house as though he owned the place, but when she had protested about it to her mother, Ruth had become tearful.

'My dear, he's been such a help—fixing everything. And you know that Daddy always thought that you and Brian . . . so it's not surprising that Brian feels he has the right——'

'Daddy never tried to pressurise me into anything,' Sylvia had said, a warning note creeping into her voice.

Lucas's deep voice cut into her thoughts. 'Something troubles you?'

She pulled herself back to the present. 'Not really.'

'No? With that frown on your face? You could have fooled me. Furthermore, I suspect it concerns Brookes.'

'Well, yes, perhaps it does in a way.' She had no wish to go into details concerning the irritations caused by Brian, who fully expected that sooner or later they would be married—but who, in the meantime, found difficulty in keeping his hands to himself. Instead she said, 'I wish Brian could afford to pay Mother the money she has in that business. Now that Daddy has gone I'd like to see her free of it.'

'Brookes has only to exercise patience and he'll have the lot.'

She was startled. 'What do you mean?'

'He'll obtain control of all the shares through you, of course. When you're married——'

'That'll be the day!' she declared furiously, then, springing to her feet, she forced a smile and took a deep breath to control her anger. 'You brought me here because you had a few words to say,' she reminded him. 'Have you said them all?'

'What I had to say somehow got out of hand. And you found a few to throw back at me. More than I expected to receive,' Lucas gritted through tight lips. 'I didn't expect this outing to affect the staff situation.'

She returned his glare, knowing he referred to the fact that she had given him notice. However, she merely gave a slight shrug and said nothing. Would he try to persuade her against her decision? she wondered. Already she was regretting it.

But apparently he had no intention of touching the subject, because he veered away from it by saying, 'I suppose it's unnecessary to tell you I'm grateful.'

Sylvia looked at him wonderingly. 'Grateful? For what? Are you saying you'll be glad to see the back of me—that you're actually *pleased* I'm leaving your—er—workforce?'

'Of course not. How can you imagine such stupidity?' he snapped. 'I mean I'm grateful to you for taking care of my aunt.'

'Even if it was without your express permission, and with the ulterior motive of creeping into your castle?' Her face remained serious. 'Shall we go now?'

She swung round and hurried away from him, tears stinging her eyes as she almost ran to where the car had been parked. But when she reached it she found it to be locked, so she had no option but to stand and wait for Lucas to arrive.

Somehow the day seemed to have lost its brightness, and as she leaned against the Alfa Romeo's white wing she began to realise she'd been too hasty in throwing his job back in his face. It was one that kept her brain pleasantly stimulated, it was well paid, and she doubted that she'd find another that satisfied her to the same extent.

She glanced across the parking area, wondering why Lucas hadn't followed her, then decided he must be browsing through some of the Tarawera eruption relics on display. Was he deliberately keeping her waiting? OK, so let him. It was quite pleasant standing beneath the trees where the birds sang in the high branches.

Her thoughts returned to her own situation, and while she told herself there were other jobs to be found—especially for one of her ability—none of them would have the added bonus of Mr Fantastic walking into the room. No other boss would have Lucas Carville's power to make her heart thump a little faster. Was it possible he would ask her to reconsider?

Again she looked across the parking area, then decided he was definitely taking his time in returning to the car. Did he expect her to go back to him? Was this his way of bringing her to heel? She bit her lip thoughtfully. Very well, perhaps she'd be wise to concede.

Leisurely she made her way back to the tea-room, but as he was not there she went outside, expecting to find him in the Buried Village. Other people were wandering about the area, which was not extensive, and it was soon obvious he was not on any of the paths, so she went towards the waterfall.

Its muted roar came to her ears, and then her hesitation was only momentary before she took careful steps down to the lower level. The track seemed steeper without the firm grip of Lucas's hand, but eventually she reached the bottom and was rewarded by the sight of his tall figure standing a short distance along the path.

She noticed he was at the place where he had kissed her, and that he appeared to be deep in thought. Nor did he turn his head until she had reached his side.

'I knew you'd come,' he said, sending her a brief smile. 'I knew I had only to wait.'

'You did?' Sylvia felt nettled. 'I wondered where you were.'

'I wanted to think—in the place where we'd stood previously.'

Before she could find a reply his arm had drawn her towards him. His head bent and as his lips found her own she became gripped by a helplessness that prevented her from exercising even the slightest willpower to resist his embrace.

She knew that for a brief moment his hand had held her breast before moving to clasp her against him, and as his pressure tightened her arms crept up to wind about his neck, almost of their own accord.

It was a long kiss that held urgent demands, and as it deepened its intensity sent her soaring into a dream world where thrushes sang among the leaves above their heads. Or was the singing in her own head, or in her heart?

Her lips parted and clear thinking became an impossibility as the fingers kneading gently along her spine sent a surge of response racing through her veins. But somewhere within the tumult of her emotions a tiny voice warned against the fire that was now threatening to burn up her control.

'Watch it—you're about to be singed!' it seemed to whisper.

Then, almost as though heaven-sent, a child came running along the path, indicating that adults were close at hand. Lucas released her abruptly and they made their way back to the parking area in silence.

CHAPTER FOUR

LITTLE was said on the journey home, and as she sat beside Lucas Sylvia waited for him to bring up the subject of her decision to leave his employment. Surely, after those kisses, he must say *something*. But he did not—and by the time they reached Sophia Street she felt thoroughly frustrated.

And then she felt even more displeased to discover Brian's car parked in the driveway. The tall fair-haired man sat in the living-room with her mother, his manner relaxed as he lounged in an easy chair. He stood up as they entered, his light blue eyes narrowing slightly as they moved from Sylvia to Lucas. 'Pleasant outing?' he enquired blandly.

'Very.' Lucas's tone was nonchalant.

Sylvia felt that something was expected of her. 'We went to Te Wairoa——'

'That must have been boring for you.' Brian's tone held derision. 'You've seen the Buried Village a hundred times. Those places are only for tourists.'

Lucas turned to her. 'Were you bored?' he asked softly, his words seeming to contain an extra question that remained unspoken.

She flashed a smile at him. 'Not at all. The afternoon definitely had highlights.' There now, she thought. That should tell him she had no real wish to leave her job. And then the memory of his kisses while being held so closely sent a flood of colour to her cheeks.

Brian's interest quickened. 'Highlights? What highlights could you possibly find in a place you've visited so often?'

A chuckle escaped Lucas. 'This will be interesting,' he drawled teasingly as he awaited Sylvia's reply.

'I'm sure it will be.' Brian's eyes were again watching her narrowly, and it seemed as if her flushed face had stirred his suspicions.

She sent him an angry glare, then took a deep breath as she said with a hint of vehemence, 'Brian Brookes, if you imagine you'll be getting a—a complete summary of the afternoon's outing, you're very much mistaken!'

His mouth became stubborn. 'I didn't ask for a complete summary. I merely asked about the highlights.'

'Well, they've now slipped my memory,' she lied.

Brian turned to Lucas. 'Perhaps you can remember them, old chap.'

Sylvia's heart skipped a beat as she sent a glance towards Lucas. Had those moments on the lower path been highlights to him? She held her breath as she awaited his reply.

But it came as an anticlimax, because he merely shrugged as he said nonchalantly, 'I don't recall much in the way of highlights. Everything seemed perfectly normal to me.'

Sylvia turned away, feeling unable to look at him. *Normal?* What did he mean by that? Normal for him to kiss a girl, she supposed. No doubt it was the beginning of a pattern he'd designed for himself. First there'd be a few kisses to open the way for closer intimacy—and later the opportunity for fulfilment would arrive.

And then Ruth's voice cut into her ponderings. Her mother had had little chance to say anything since their arrival home, and Sylvia wondered if she now sensed the tension that had crept into the atmosphere. However, her words seemed to brush away the growing friction as she spoke to Lucas.

'Brian and I have been chatting over business affairs,' she told him. 'I've invited him to stay for the evening meal. I hope you'll join us. I know your aunt would be pleased to see more of you this evening.'

'Thank you, but I've no wish to impose——'

'Especially as you've already had lunch here,' Brian said pointedly, his jaw tightening.

Ruth laughed. 'Don't be selfish, Brian. You know you have meals here almost every weekend.'

'Only because there are usually agency affairs to discuss,' he defended. 'If Sylvia were back in the office you'd know more about the state of the business.'

Lucas sent him a questioning glance. 'I trust all is going well in that direction?'

'Its direction is not your concern,' snapped Brian, his irritation more than obvious.

Ruth said quickly, 'Be sensible, Brian. It could be helpful to discuss matters with Lucas. His aunt has been telling me how very successful he's become.'

Brian's mouth twisted into a sneer. 'Oh, yes—the castle-builder,' he said scathingly.

Ruth glared at him coldly, an angry flush rising to her cheeks. 'You're being rude to my guest, Brian,' she snapped. 'If you're not careful I'll rescind that invitation and ask you to leave!'

Brian maintained a sulky silence for several moments before he said, 'Carville knows perfectly well how things are in the business world. He'll be well aware that property sales are rather slow at the present. It's the state of the economy, of course.'

Lucas said crisply, 'The state of the economy makes a handy excuse for numerous situations.'

'What's that supposed to mean?' snarled Brian.

'Nothing specific—except that my only interest in that real estate business would be the knowledge that Ruth receives a fair interest on the money she has invested in it.'

Brian swung round to focus on Sylvia. 'Been chatting, have you? Gossiping about your mother's private affairs and no doubt suggesting she receives a poor rate of interest?'

She opened her mouth to protest, but before she could deny the accusation Lucas came to her rescue by speaking to Brian.

'Interest rates are fairly good at present. Naturally, I have no idea of her situation, but if she isn't getting a suitable return, I could get it for her—providing she can get her money out of the agency, of course.'

Brian drew a sharp breath, then gritted, 'Ruth will thank you to mind your own damned business!'

Lucas grinned at him. 'She will? Then she herself will have to convince me on that point.' Brushing the subject aside, he turned to Sylvia. 'Come, it's time we went in to see Amy.'

They found his aunt lying snugly in bed, her head raised by pillows. She greeted them with a smile as she said to Sylvia, 'I was so glad when your mother told me you'd gone out together. Was it a pleasant afternoon?'

'Yes, very pleasant,' Sylvia assured her.

'With highlights,' grinned Lucas.

'How are you feeling?' Sylvia asked hastily before this statement could be explained further.

'Much better than when you wrapped me up and brought me here. I suppose the antibiotics are beginning to show effect—to say nothing of your mother's care and attention.'

'You'll weary yourself if you talk too much,' Lucas warned.

'But I want to talk. I want to tell everyone that Ruth is simply wonderful. She knows exactly what to do.'

'That's not surprising,' Sylvia explained. 'During her nursing days she became matron of a small private hospital, but after I came along she devoted her time to Daddy and me.'

Amy said, 'She's told me about your father and the reason for turning her home into a place of convalescence. And of course I've told her about my poor dear Joe——' The words ended with a sigh.

'You appear to have clicked into a friendship,' Lucas observed.

'Yes, I think you can be sure of that.' Amy's eyes turned to Sylvia. 'I'm so thankful you came to work for Lucas.'

Lucas uttered clipped words. 'Unfortunately the job will be short-lived. Isn't that so?' He grinned at Sylvia.

Amy's eyes widened as she turned to him. 'What do you mean?'

'I'm saying that Sylvia has already handed in her notice. She'll be leaving us in two weeks.'

Amy made no effort to conceal her dismay. 'Oh, I am sorry about that.' She turned to Sylvia. 'Aren't you happy working for Lucas?'

Sylvia bit her lip, unable to find words.

Amy went on vehemently, 'Don't tell me you've come up against the Ransom already?'

Lucas cut in, his tone ironical. 'It has nothing to do with Maureen. As yet they haven't even met. It's Sylvia's own decision.'

Amy sighed. 'Well, I can only say I'm most disappointed.' Then, as a thought struck her, 'You have a better job to go to?'

'Indeed she has,' Lucas informed his aunt. 'And possibly it's a job she should never have left.'

Sylvia turned to stare at him. 'What are you talking about?'

'Naturally, you'll be racing back to Brian. The proverbial homing pigeon returning to the nest.'

'You couldn't be more wrong!' she flashed at him, her spirits descending to a low level. The hard note in his voice indicated he had no intention of persuading her to change her mind, nor would her own pride allow her to suggest she had any wish to do so.

Further, she had a sudden suspicion he was glad she would be leaving, his lack of any visible regret making her feel sure it was almost a relief for him to know that within a short time she would be out of his sight and away from the vicinity of his office.

Another sigh came from the older woman in the bed. 'I wish I knew why you've made this decision,' she said, gazing earnestly at Sylvia. 'You've been with Lucas for such a short time, and he's been so pleased with everything you've done. Maureen had got behind with the work, but you've caught up with it all. I know, because he's told me how efficient you are.'

'I've tried to do my best,' murmured Sylvia, secretly glowing from the praise, although it also confirmed her suspicions. Despite her capability, wild horses wouldn't force him to ask her to stay.

Almost as though reading her thoughts, Amy turned to Lucas. 'Can't you persuade her to change her mind?'

His voice had a ring of granite. 'I never persuade people to do anything against their will. It won't be the first time a person has left me standing in the rain,' he added ironically.

Amy frowned. 'The rain? I don't understand, dear. Are you saying the roof leaks?'

He laughed. 'Of course not. I mean out in the cold. It's just a metaphor, Aunt.'

'He's good at metaphors,' Sylvia explained.

'Is he, indeed?' retorted Amy. 'This one makes him sound as if he's sorry for himself. Well, I can't say I blame him. I'm sure that losing you will be a blow.'

'One becomes accustomed to such blows,' Lucas assured his aunt.

His meaning pierced Sylvia's mind. So that was it! Her rejection of him years ago had again reared its head. It still rankled, and when she had appeared in his office he had accepted her in the job only because he was in dire need of her services. Forcing a smile, she said to

Amy, 'He'll manage very well without me. Maureen will be back at work tomorrow.'

Amy looked at her intently. 'Please excuse an old woman's curiosity, but—when you leave, have you plans for another job?'

Sylvia searched for words, then made a spur-of-the-moment decision as she grasped at an idea. 'I've been forced to realise that it's my duty to take a look at the real estate office.'

'She means she's going back to Brian,' Lucas said drily.

Amy continued to eye her intently. 'He's the young man your father took in as a partner? Your mother told me about him.'

'Yes. He's always moaning about the lack of business, and I feel I'd be wise to examine the situation for myself. You see, Mother's finances are involved, and on her behalf I'd like to see exactly how well Brian is running the business.'

Amy gave her an understanding nod. 'Very wise—although I'm sorry it's forcing you to leave Lucas.' She paused, then added shrewdly, 'Of course, you know that Lucas could make all these enquiries for you.'

'Yes, I suppose so—but he's really too busy to be concerned with my affairs. To be honest, I'd prefer to look into them myself.'

'What you really have in mind is a spot of private spying,' Lucas said, his amusement thinly disguised.

The suggestion appalled her. 'Spying is a horrible word,' she protested. 'Surely I have the right to learn the true situation?'

'You're quite right, my dear,' Amy said unexpectedly. 'Your first duty is to watch over your mother's affairs. Lucas can't expect to have everything his own way, and after all, he has *Maureen*.'

'I'll bet he has!' Sylvia flashed, then immediately regretted the words.

Lucas sent her a look of enquiry. 'Do I detect antagonism towards a person you've never met?'

'Of course not,' she said with as much control as she could muster. What was the matter with her, for Pete's sake?

Amy turned to Lucas. 'I've often wondered if you've thought of taking Maureen into partnership. I know she has a degree of some kind.'

Her words gave Sylvia a shock, but she managed to nod with understanding and to say sweetly, 'You mean someone with whom to share his castle?'

Amy betrayed surprise. 'He's told you about that? He's usually very secretive about it. It's one of those little jokes known only to the inner circle of the family.'

Sylvia smiled. 'Apparently not any longer, because Maureen also knows about it.'

Amy betrayed surprise, her eyes widening as she exclaimed, 'Well, you do amaze me!' She turned to Lucas as though awaiting further explanation.

He scowled. 'I'm afraid it became necessary for me to tell her about it,' he admitted with reluctance.

Again Amy showed surprise. '*Necessary* to confide in her?' She paused, regarding him thoughtfully. 'I can only imagine you must think a lot of her to have done so. Far more than I realised——'

'It was forced upon me,' he explained with infinite patience. 'It happened one day when Grandfather came storming into the office. He was in a fine rage because one of his investments had gone wrong and he demanded to see me. Maureen happened to be near the reception desk and she told him I was too busy to see anyone.'

'Didn't she know he was your grandfather?' asked Amy.

'Not at that time, because it was during her early days with me. He told her that if she didn't drag me down from the battlements he'd clamber up the tower himself.'

Amy laughed weakly. 'I can just hear him!'

'Later I could see she considered him to be a raving lunatic, so I thought I'd better explain his remarks.'

Amy sighed. 'Poor old Grandfather, his temper did nothing to help his blood-pressure. I'm glad you haven't inherited it.'

'We're different,' Lucas retorted crisply. 'When Grandfather got mad he used to burst forth, whereas I'm inclined to keep it bottled inside me.'

Sylvia turned to Amy. 'He means that he allows it to simmer and cause resentment for *years*.'

'Then he's unwise,' Amy commented. 'It's much better to burst out and get rid of anger. Constant bitterness can poison the soul.'

Lucas sent Sylvia a look that was definitely cool. 'Are you trying to tell me something about myself?'

'Nothing that you don't already know,' she informed him calmly.

Amy's voice came from the bed. 'Getting back to my suggestion of a partnership with Maureen——'

Lucas raised dark brows. 'Yes? You were actually serious?'

'Why would I joke about such a matter? After all, Maureen has been with you a few years now. She's an attractive woman and so very efficient. I'm sure you'd hate to be without her.'

Lucas regarded his aunt with amused tolerance. 'This is a new trend of thought for you, Aunt. Are you really saying you think it would be a wise move?'

'Well, yes, in many ways.' She was suddenly hesitant until she declared with more decision, 'At least it would prevent her from leaving you—and you know you *need* her.'

'Then I'd better give it my serious consideration.'

Sylvia looked from one to the other. Was she really hearing this conversation which seemed to be so calculated and cold-blooded? Yet she sensed the wisdom in

Amy's suggestion which would give Maureen an extra interest in the business, thus making it less likely for her to leave—as she herself intended doing. So why should the thought niggle at her?

Almost as though reading her thoughts, Amy sent her a direct look as she said pointedly, 'It's so disappointing for Lucas when girls who are so competent leave him—not that it happens very often.'

The words made Sylvia feel guilty. She realised that now was her opportunity to climb off her high horse—to capitulate and say she would stay in the job. In fact she wondered vaguely if Amy had attempted to push this thought into her mind.

But again pride kept her silent. She'd stay only if Lucas asked her to do so—and at the present moment this prospect appeared to be most unlikely.

And then the blessed interruption occurred when Ruth came into the room with Amy's evening meal. It was set on a tray with legs, and as Amy raised herself in the bed it was placed before her.

Ruth plumped the pillows behind Amy's back. Cheerfully she said, 'Brian is pouring drinks in the living-room, and when a certain lady is off her antibiotics she'll be able to join us in a sherry.'

Amy said, 'You treat us too well. That Mr Mackenzie came in to chat this afternoon. He was singing your praises.'

Ruth laughed. 'That's only because of the wee dram I provide each evening. Poor man, he's suffered with his hips——'

Amy looked at her nephew. 'Lucas dear, I'd be grateful if you'd give Ruth a cheque on my behalf.'

Ruth uttered a quick protest. 'No, thank you—there's to be no payment from Amy.'

The dark brows rose. 'Oh? Why not, may I ask?' demanded Lucas.

'Because she didn't apply to come here as a convalescent patient,' Ruth explained. 'She was invited here by Sylvia, and that puts her into the category of being a guest. There's a difference, you understand.'

Lucas turned to Sylvia, his eyes full of thinly veiled questions. 'I wonder if I do—understand.'

'I doubt it,' she told him flatly, guessing that he referred to his earlier suggestion that she could have had a reason for putting his aunt in her mother's care—a motive that could place her closer to his own side. Nor did she betray her irritation. Instead she sent him a singularly sweet smile as she said, 'No doubt you'll make up your own mind in due course.'

Almost as though sensing a growing tension between them, Ruth said, 'If we don't return to the living-room Jock Mackenzie will be growing agitated for his meal.'

Lucas spoke seriously. 'You'll excuse me if I leave soon after it. Maureen will be back at work on Monday and there's work to be done on an auditing task I'm preparing for her.'

'A task I'm unable to do?' Sylvia asked almost reproachfully.

'Only because I haven't had sufficient time to lay it before you,' he explained. 'Also, Maureen has done it before.'

Amy said brightly, 'He has such confidence in Maureen. He'd be wise to consider that partnership suggestion.'

Sylvia became conscious of a deep despondency. Confidence in Maureen, she thought, but not in herself. Nor was this state of affairs surprising. Maureen, who had been with him for so long, had everything at her fingertips, while she herself had already proved her own unreliability by giving notice within such a short time. But he knew what had caused her to do so, didn't he? Surely it was up to him to make amends? Or was he deliberately allowing her to stew in her own juice?

Also, despite her assertions of looking into the affairs at the real estate agency, it must be more than obvious to Lucas that this had been a spur-of-the-moment decision, otherwise she would have taken a job there instead of with him. Well, the weekend was not yet over. Perhaps he would come tomorrow and ask her to change her mind.

But Sunday passed without a sign of him, not even to see his aunt. And Sylvia, who had put on one of her more attractive dresses, found difficulty in hiding her disappointment.

'Perhaps he's visiting Maureen,' said Amy without looking at Sylvia. 'Perhaps he's discussing—what I suggested—away from the office where there could be interruptions.'

'Yes—perhaps,' Sylvia responded in a dull voice, although the thought of Lucas taking in a partner did not correspond with what she now felt to be his nature. He was an independent do-it-himself type of person, and to suddenly share what he had personally built was hardly characteristic of him.

Next morning Sylvia's sense of depression was even deeper. Nor did the reason for its continual presence take long to manifest itself, and as she lay gazing at the ceiling she realised that today she would meet Maureen Ransom for the first time.

So why should this concern her? If it had not been for the influenza that had been so prevalent during the last months of winter, Maureen would not have been laid low. And if it hadn't been for Maureen's illness the job would not have arisen. The employment agency would not have sent her to Lucas Carville—nor would she have come face to face with the man she had rejected seven years ago.

Her mind flew back to that day at Waiotapu when they had stood near the Bridal Veil Falls. His proposal had come as a shock, mainly because, being so young and inexperienced, she hadn't taken him seriously. In fact, she had taken it as a joke, and her laughter had risen over the muted roar of the falls. Now she almost cringed as she recalled the stricken look on his face.

But at the time he too had been inexperienced—an entirely different individual from the man with whom she had shared moments of closeness on the path below the Buried Village at Te Wairoa. The latter was a man with expertise who knew how to stir with kisses that made her nerves tingle and sent her blood racing through her veins.

A smile touched her lips while the memory of his arms holding her close to his body made her feel hot. Did the pressure of his lips betray the growing passion that caused his breath to quicken? Of course it did—and then a tremor passed through her as she recalled her own response.

At the same time a question raised its head. Had those kisses contained any real depth of meaning for Lucas? Little was needed to indicate that he had never forgiven her for rejecting him—so was he merely leading her down an emotional garden path for the sake of revenge?

Her eyes narrowed and suddenly she felt cold as she considered this as a reason for his embrace; and the more she thought about it, the more certain she became that he intended making a bid for her affections—and then he would reject her. It would be sweet revenge indeed.

Incensed, she raised her right hand and spoke aloud. 'OK, Lucas Carville, I can follow the trend of your thoughts. The next time you dare to make a pass at me you'll get short shrift! Just you wait and see, Lucas Carville!'

And with this decision firmly fixed in her mind she sprang out of bed, showered, then dressed in the conservative navy suit she had worn on her first day at the office. There was something about its deep blue colour and contrasting pale pink blouse that gave her confidence, perhaps because it made her hair look even more blonde, and this morning she needed all the confidence she could find.

She reached the office a little earlier than usual, a quick glance showing the Alfa Romeo to be already in the private car park at the rear of the building. However, there was no need to go near Lucas for instructions, because there was still a pile of work waiting beside the computer.

Vaguely, she heard the subdued chatter of Karen and June, coupled with giggles from the latter, until a more dominant voice told them to get on with their work. There was instant silence, and Sylvia froze as she realised the Ransom was back at work.

Moments later the same voice spoke from behind her. 'I suppose you're Sylvia Sinclair.'

She turned to face a tall, slim woman whose light brown hair framed features that were not unattractive. The grey eyes set beneath straight brows were shadowed by lashes heavy with mascara, while an effort had been made to improve the thin lips by a generous application of glossy lipstick.

Sylvia forced a friendly smile. 'Yes—and I suppose you're Maureen. I hope you're feeling better.'

'Quite, thank you. And incidentally, I'm Miss Ransom to the staff.' The lips thinned as she took in every inch of Sylvia's appearance, then her voice became cool as she said, 'I'll have you know you're using my computer. I'll continue with that work and we'll find something else for you to do on the other computer. It's not quite as up-to-date as this one, but it'll be suitable for anything you have to do.'

Sylvia made no effort to move as she said, 'This job was given to me by Lucas, so I'll continue until he takes me off it.'

Maureen's eyes turned to pebbles. '*Lucas?* How long, may I ask, have you been calling Mr Carville *Lucas*?'

Sylvia shrugged. 'Ever since I first met him seven years ago.'

'*Seven——?*' Maureen's jaw sagged slightly, her eyes widened, then narrowed thoughtfully as they rested on Sylvia's blonde hair. 'I think I've heard of you,' she said softly.

'Oh?' Sylvia felt a sudden apprehension. Surely Lucas had never spoken of their earlier association to Maureen?

But the latter's next words came as a surprise. 'Aren't you the Sylvia who's friendly with Brian Brookes?'

'Yes, I suppose you could say we're—friendly.' The admission came guardedly.

'I always liked Brian—he's such a *dear* man,' Maureen enthused.

'Is he? I hadn't noticed.'

'Was it your father with whom he was in partnership? But now I understand he owns the business.'

'Not quite,' Sylvia's words came drily.

'What do you mean by *not quite*? Of course he owns it. He told me so—and if he *says* he owns it, well, *of course* he owns it.'

Sylvia had no intention of going into details, so she merely said, 'I think you'll find he's exaggerating.'

'I doubt it.' Maureen's tone had become superior.

'Really? Do you know him well?'

'I've known him ever since schooldays, although we don't see very much of each other.' The grey eyes regarded Sylvia curiously as she asked, 'How well do *you* know Brian?'

'Well enough to doubt much of what he says.' And then further discussion was brushed aside as Sylvia recalled Lucas's words of the previous evening. 'I think Lucas has a special job for you to begin. Perhaps you should learn what he has in mind.' And having offered that advice she turned back to her work, although she was well aware that Maureen paused to stare at her intently before leaving the room.

Sylvia had no further contact with Maureen before the morning tea break, and then the senior's thinly veiled antagonism towards her was impossible to miss. As she walked into the kitchen she knew the grey eyes swept her from head to foot, and while she sipped her tea she felt Maureen watching her from across the top of her cup. Instinct warned that a complaint was on the way, yet when it emerged it took her by surprise.

Still watching her closely, Maureen said, 'I believe you were taken out to lunch on your very first day here.'

'Really?' Sylvia kept her tone noncommittal.

'Well, is it true?' The question was snapped.

'Yes, it's true. So what?'

Maureen spoke sharply. 'You'd better understand that I don't approve of staff socialising with the boss, so don't imagine you'll be making a habit of it.' Her eyes rested on the pink blouse ruffles snuggling against the smoothness of Sylvia's throat, then her voice became cold as she demanded, 'Where did he take you? Somewhere special, I suppose.'

'Not at all. Only to Waiotapu.'

Maureen gasped. 'Only to—but that's miles away! The lunch hour must have been well stretched!'

'He often takes people to Waiotapu,' Karen put in.

Maureen glared at her. 'Visitors who are strangers to Rotorua. But Sylvia doesn't come into that category.' The shadowed grey eyes became full of questions as they returned to Sylvia.

It was necessary to find an answer, so she gave a small shrug and said vaguely, 'Oh—we reminisced.'

'About what?' The question was snapped somewhat rudely.

Sylvia kept a rein on her temper. She had no wish to quarrel with Maureen on the first morning of their acquaintance, so she lied and said casually, 'I've really forgotten. If you're so very interested, why don't you ask

Lucas? It's possible he'd remember our conversation—that's if it's any concern of yours, of course.'

Maureen's lips thinned. 'I'm merely pointing out that it's unwise to become too friendly with the boss. It usually leads to embarrassment on both sides, and of course ends with dismissal.'

'So if I'm invited to lunch again I must refuse?'

'I'd advise it,' Maureen snapped crisply.

'Am I to understand you're dictating my private life as well as my office hours?' Sylvia demanded drily.

'I didn't say that——'

'And I can presume that on these grounds you yourself would refuse an invitation to lunch with Lucas?'

The question was followed by a tense silence while Maureen sought for an answer—until suddenly the quietness in the room was broken by an outburst of giggles from June.

It brought a reaction of anger. 'Get back to your reception desk!' Maureen snapped at the junior. 'You've overstepped the time for your tea break. You can wash the cups later.'

'Yes, Miss Ransom,' June muttered demurely. 'But I must say this particular break sure has been interesting!' And with that brief remark she vanished, closely followed by Karen.

Maureen swung round to glare at Sylvia. 'I trust I've made myself clear?'

'Not really. I still don't know if your—advice—is to be followed by you, or only by me. Nor can I understand why you're so uptight over something that happened a fortnight ago, and is unlikely to happen again.'

'How can I be sure of that?' The question came coldly.

'Because I won't be here. I've given notice.'

Maureen's jaw sagged. 'You have? For what reason would you give notice after such a short time?'

'That's not your business—nor do I intend to go into details. However, sooner or later you'd learn that I'm leaving, so you might as well be told now.'

Maureen took a deep breath, then her voice shook slightly. 'Don't tell me he made a pass at you?'

'Not in the way you mean.'

'Well then, in what way?'

Sylvia became exasperated. 'Kindly mind your own business, Maureen. It has nothing to do with you.'

'At least you're not leaving because of me.'

'Of course not. You may be able to bully Karen and June, but on me you have no effect whatever.'

And with that parting shot she returned to the computer, where the necessary concentration did much to calm her emotions. At least they remained calm until she paused to reflect that she would now be working in this office for only a limited period. After that she would again lose contact with Lucas—which was something to be regretted.

CHAPTER FIVE

It was her own fault, Sylvia told herself as she gazed sightlessly at the computer screen. Her own impetuosity had caused her to give notice without due consideration. Yet, however much she reviewed the situation, she knew she could not work for a man who believed his castle of success had caused her to come to heel.

Nor did she catch more than a passing sight of him during the rest of that day, and when she left the office she felt despondent. However, when she arrived home her depression was brushed aside when she discovered the number three bedroom to be occupied, and that her mother needed assistance with the evening meal.

'I'll attend to Mrs Grayson,' she offered.

'Thank you, dear,' said Ruth. 'It's ready to be served. Just put it on the tray and take it in to her.'

'How is she?'

'Improving all the time, but I'm not allowing her out of this place until she's really well.'

'You'll keep her in bed?'

'Only until she's well enough to get out of it. It isn't good for older people to lie in bed unnecessarily. It's better for them to be up and moving about. However, she'll not leave that bed until I say so.'

Sylvia laughed. 'Dear Mother, you do love to be the boss!'

'Only when I know what's good for a person.'

'Somehow you usually do know,' Sylvia agreed. She paused as a thought struck her. 'You haven't yet told me who's in number three.'

Ruth chuckled, sending her a side glance. 'I've been waiting for you to ask—nor would you ever guess.'

'Oh?' Sylvia was only mildly interested.

'It's Ellen Brookes.'

Mild interest turned to deep dismay. 'You mean—Brian's mother?'

'Who else? The poor woman had a fall. It seems she tripped over the vacuum cleaner while in the bedroom. She landed against the sharp edge of the dressing-table and damaged her ribs.'

'They're—fractured?'

'Fortunately, no. Brian found her when he went home for lunch. She was almost unable to move, so he phoned a doctor, who arranged for her to be X-rayed. She's been told she must rest until she can move without pain, and, frankly, she has little option to do otherwise.'

'Which means going to bed,' said Sylvia.

'That's right. Brian phoned to ask if I could take care of her.'

'Naturally you agreed.'

'Would you have had me turn her away?'

'Of course not—only it means he'll be in and out of this house *ad nauseam*. It'll give him the excuse to almost take up residence!'

'You're exaggerating, dear,' said Ruth. 'In any case, it won't be for long—probably a week at the most.'

'That'll be plenty.'

Sylvia sighed as she turned towards the kitchen, and while she set the tray for Amy Grayson her thoughts were directed mainly towards Ellen Brookes. On the rare occasion she had come in contact with Brian's tall, thin mother she had sensed the latter's disapproval of her. It had taken the form of a lofty superiority in her attitude, and Sylvia could only presume it was because she had had the utter temerity to refuse Brian's offer of marriage.

It hadn't taken long for her to realise that Brian was his mother's darling, the one who had remained with her when she had divorced her husband many years ago. So it was only natural for his mother to believe that Brian should have whatever he considered to be necessary for his happiness. Well, she herself was not on that particular list, and the sooner they realised it the better.

Brushing Brian and his mother from her mind, she picked up the tray and carried it into the number one bedroom, where Amy Grayson lay propped against the pillows.

The hazel eyes lit as they watched Sylvia adjust the tray legs and remove the plate cover. 'Thank you, dear—that looks appetising.'

'Then I hope you'll eat every scrap.'

'I'll do that—even if it hastens my recovery and forces my return to that lonely house above the lake.'

'It has a magnificent view,' Sylvia pointed out.

'No doubt, but having seen the view numerous times one reaches the stage of no longer looking at it. That house needs love and laughter within the walls, rather than a view that's away in the distance. One is warm, the other is cold.'

'I suppose the house is rather large for only two people,' Sylvia agreed thoughtfully.

'It was built with a family in mind,' Amy explained. 'But Lucas's grandfather had only one son. It broke the old man's heart when his son and my sister were killed. Their deaths turned him into an irascible type of person who declared he'd been cheated by life.' She paused, then looked at Sylvia with a gleam of questions in her eyes. 'Well now, how did your day go? Tell me about it.'

'There's little to tell. It was busy as usual.'

'Maureen is back at work?' The query came casually.

'Yes.'

'She should lighten the load. How did you get along with her?'

Sylvia gave a small shrug. 'I saw so little of her.'

'But you must have seen something of Lucas.' The hazel eyes became penetrating.

'I doubt that I saw him at all.'

'Closeted with Maureen, was he?'

'I've no idea.' Sylvia watched the older woman enjoying the food placed before her, then was unable to resist a question. 'Were you serious when you suggested he should take Maureen in as a partner?'

'As a working partner—yes.' Amy sent Sylvia a direct look. 'Obviously he needs somebody he can rely on, someone who's unlikely to leave him for another job——'

'As I'm about to do,' Sylvia added for her.

Amy dabbed her lips with a table napkin as she said, 'His *real* need lies in a marriage partnership with someone who'll give him love and comfort.'

'You have Maureen in mind for that job?' Sylvia asked doubtfully.

Amy poured cream on her dessert. 'Certainly not! I suspect that Maureen is concerned mainly with Maureen, whereas Lucas needs someone who can *give*—lovingly.'

'I can see you have his interests at heart,' said Sylvia drily.

'What else would you expect? He's been like a son to me.'

What else, indeed? Sylvia questioned mentally. And along the passage was another woman who demanded the best for her son. Did mothers ever consider the needs of the girl their precious son wanted to marry? Was any daughter-in-law ever good enough for any mother's son? Somehow she doubted it.

Amy's voice cut into her thoughts. 'I hope Lucas will come to see me this evening. Mr Mackenzie says that Lucas is what he'd call a bonny laddie.'

Sylvia laughed, then attempted a Scottish accent. 'Aye, he is that—a bonny laddie.'

But Amy remained serious as she sent her an enquiring look. 'Is it possible that you also consider him to be a bonny laddie?'

'I'd be a liar if I denied it,' Sylvia admitted frankly. 'At work Karen and June refer to him as Mr Fantastic.'

'And you, my dear?' The question came softly. 'Would you turn him down, as that other girl did seven years ago?'

Sylvia felt an inner shock. Did Amy *know* she was that same girl? Had Lucas confided in her? Somehow it seemed unlikely. 'How could I possibly answer such a question?' she prevaricated, then brushed it away by adding lightly, 'In any case, it's good manners to wait until one is asked.'

And this, Sylvia realised, was something else that was most unlikely. Hadn't Lucas assured her that any emotional feelings he had had for her in the past were now dead and buried.

It was mid-evening before he arrived. Dinner was over, the dishes had been put through the dishwasher and the three convalescents had been settled for the night.

By that time Amy had become fretful with disappointment. 'He's not coming,' she complained.

'Give him time,' Sylvia consoled while hiding her own disappointment. 'He's probably been busy finding a meal for himself.'

'That's almost correct.' Lucas's voice spoke from the bedroom doorway while the dark eyes took in the care with which Sylvia had arranged Amy's pillows.

'Where have you been?' Amy demanded.

'In a restaurant with Maureen,' he told her nonchalantly.

'With—with Maureen——?' The echo came faintly from the bed.

'Yes. I thought you'd be pleased.' His expression had become sardonic. 'We had several matters to discuss, so we did it over a meal.'

Amy's smile appeared to be forced. 'How—how nice for you——'

'And for Maureen,' Sylvia was unable to resist adding, inwardly amused as she recalled their conversation at morning tea-break. 'It would confirm your delight in having her back at work.'

'Of course he's delighted,' Amy echoed. She turned to Lucas. 'Have you given any thought to my suggestion?'

A cautious note crept into his voice. 'What suggestion was that, Amy? I don't really recall——'

'About a partnership with Maureen, of course.'

'Oh, *that*. Well, yes, I've given it thought.'

'And——?' The hazel eyes watched him intently.

'No decision at present. These matters are not to be rushed.'

Sylvia added hastily. 'I'll leave you to discuss it. Perhaps Amy will be able to persuade you.'

His face became expressionless as he turned to her. 'Do you also think it would be a good idea—I mean, now that you've met her?'

'Only if it would remove the inconvenience of losing competent staff,' she admitted after a moment's hesitation.

'You're forgetting that staff can be replaced.'

She sent him a direct look. 'That's something I never forget. Nobody is indispensable,' she said pointedly, then wondered if he'd got the message. To drive it home she added, 'Even you yourself have climbed over the disappointments of years ago.'

'You mean like—seven years ago?'

'That's right. And if you're honest you'll admit it,' she said, smiling to soften the words as she disappeared through the door.

It was an hour before Lucas left his aunt's bedside, and when he entered the living-room his tightened jaw indicated a barely concealed displeasure.

Sylvia observed the scowl on the dark brow, then wondered if an argument with Amy had taken place. Or was he irritated by the sight of Brian lounging at ease in an armchair.

The latter did not bother to rise or offer any form of greeting to Lucas. Instead he continued in earnest conversation with Ruth, who politely silenced him as she turned to the tall, dark man with a question. 'Do you think Amy is looking better?'

Lucas gave a short laugh. 'Definitely better. She's now well enough to pass strong opinions on what I should be doing with my business—and with my life. Is she on a new type of drug—something that's gone to her head and loosened her tongue?'

'There's been no change of pills,' Ruth assured him gravely. 'She has yet to finish the course prescribed by the doctor.'

Sylvia said quickly, 'Who's for coffee? I'm about to make some.'

Lucas nodded. 'Thank you, that would be enjoyable.'

Brian stood up, declaring assertively, 'I'll help you.'

'No, thank you, I can do it alone,' Sylvia assured him firmly.

Ruth said, 'Sit down, Brian. I want to hear more about the state of the business, and you've told me so little. It's almost as though you imagine I've lost interest in the place.'

A shade of annoyance crossed Brian's face, but it vanished immediately as he sat down again and began to elaborate on property sales during the last three months.

Sylvia breathed a silent vote of thanks towards her mother. She went to the kitchen, but had no sooner taken coffee-mugs from their hooks when she turned to discover that Lucas had followed her.

He said, 'I told them I felt sure their conversation would be confidential and that I would help you.'

'That was diplomatic, even if you're unable to do much in the way of help.'

'I can at least carry the tray,' he pointed out, watching her put flat iced Belgium biscuits on a plate. 'Could Brookes do more than that?'

'He could annoy me by not keeping his hands to himself,' she retorted with more force than she intended.

'In that case I'd be wise to keep mine in my pockets.'

He was still in a sombre mood, she noticed as she decided to make no reply to that particular remark. However, she was conscious of her own spirits rising at the thought of having these few minutes alone with him.

'He's definitely very much at home in this house,' he observed. 'Does he—er—pay court every evening?'

Sylvia ignored his sardonic tone as she replied, 'I suppose we can expect him during the coming week. His mother is now in room three.' She went on to explain the accident sustained by Mrs Brookes. 'So you see I'm not the reason for this evening's visit,' she finished drily.

'Ah, but you must admit you're the reason on most other occasions.'

She turned to face him. 'I can't understand why you're so sure I'm the only girl in Brian's life.'

The dark brows rose. 'You're saying he has other girlfriends?'

'Plenty of them. I'm merely the one who could advantage him the most—at least I was when Daddy was alive, but now that's changed because he has control of the business—apart from Mother's shares, of course.'

'Which he'd like to see transferred to his own name?' Lucas suggested shrewdly.

'That's right.'

'Has he offered to buy them from her?'

'Yes—for a pittance. Mother told him she had no intention of actually giving them to him but that she'd consider——' Sylvia fell silent as her tongue almost ran away with her.

Lucas grinned and finished the sentence for her. 'But that she'd consider giving them to you as a wedding present when you decided to marry. Isn't that what you were going to say?'

'Something like that,' she admitted reluctantly. 'How did you guess?'

'Because it's the sort of thing that mothers do. She'd sacrifice her own income from the shares to give you a small amount of money of your own.'

'Well, I dislike the thought of such a situation. Nor have I any intention of being married for a bundle of shares. They've built a wall between us.'

He leaned against the bench, his arms folded across his broad chest. 'You're fooling yourself,' he told her.

'What do you mean?'

'I can see the picture quite clearly. It's not the thought of the shares that bugs you, it's the knowledge that he has other female friends.'

'Rubbish! I couldn't care less about them,' Sylvia snapped.

'You fear they'll always be there——'

'Nonsense! I don't give them a thought——'

'In fact the picture becomes even clearer. *They* are the reason you left the agency office and sought other jobs,' Lucas persisted.

She almost stamped a foot as anger gripped her. 'You're talking absolute rot! It wasn't like that at all.'

He set his jaw. 'I think it was.'

'Then you're a *fool*. It's difficult to believe you can be so—so *stupid*!' Her voice had begun to shake.

'Go steady with those insults! I'm still your boss, you know.'

'Not for much longer!' she flashed at him, then, controlling her irritation, she said, 'If we don't take this coffee into the living room it'll be cold.

She lifted the tray, but Lucas took it from her, then waited for her to precede him to where Ruth and Brian were still discussing the estate agency affairs. Fortunately they were too engrossed to notice the angry flush that continued to hover in Sylvia's cheeks.

In an effort to give them further privacy she carried her coffee out to the veranda. Lucas followed her, and together they stood in a patch of moonlight. Would he tell her about the discussion with Maureen? she wondered. To set the subject in motion she said, 'I hope Maureen wasn't too tired after her first day back at work.'

'She didn't complain.' The words came abruptly.

She waited for more to come, but he merely inhaled deeply and said, 'There's a pleasant perfume coming from somewhere.'

'It's the pink boronia bush beside the veranda steps.'

His remark was enough to tell her he had no intention of satisfying her curiosity. Nor did it seem as if he had any intention of remaining close to her, because he moved to the veranda rail where he stood gazing across the moonlit garden.

'You look as if you're waiting for someone,' she remarked.

'Why do you say that?'

'There's an air of expectancy about you.'

'You're surprisingly sensitive.' Lucas paused, then without looking at her he asked, 'Have you ever waited for someone to appear—waited for someone who doesn't come near?'

'No. Nor would I. I'd go out and find the person in question. Naturally, it would depend on the extent of my longing to catch up with the aforesaid party——'

'You make it sound very easy,' he observed.

'I would have thought that most things were easy for Lucas Carville. Another mug of coffee?'

'No, thank you.'

'Of course, if you're waiting for someone to—*come to heel*—you'll probably wait a long time.'

Ruefully, he said, 'Grandfather had a down-to-earth way of expressing himself. I didn't expect you to take his opinion so personally.'

'I'm not concerned with your grandfather's opinion. It's your own that has come through so loud and clear.'

'My opinion is of importance to you?'

'Of course. You're my boss, as you reminded me—at least until the end of the week,' Sylvia added, giving him the opportunity to say something about that particular situation.

But he did not. Instead he handed her his empty mug and said, 'It's time I went home. Thank you for the coffee. See you tomorrow.'

Disappointed, she watched him descend the steps rapidly, then stride to where the Alfa Romeo had been left on the drive. Lights blazed as he backed towards the street, and then there was only the moonlight and the silence which gave her the eerie feeling he had not been there at all.

By the time Sylvia went to bed that night she felt thoroughly disgruntled. Somehow the day seemed to have gone badly until it had ended with harsh words between Lucas and herself, and as she lay between the sheets she realised she had no wish for antagonism to simmer between them. The remainder of her time in his office would be short enough, so for heaven's sake let it be pleasant.

But the next day did not pass as smoothly as she could have hoped, the trouble beginning when morning tea-break was almost over.

June was the one who started it off. She appeared to be bubbling with an inner excitement, and eventually she was unable to control her tongue. Sending Maureen an arch smile, she said brightly, 'Gosh, Miss Ransom, I was surprised to see you out with the boss last night—especially so soon after ordering Sylvia not to accept an invitation if he happened to ask her out.'

Maureen glared at the younger girl. '*Ordered?* What are you talking about? I merely advised——'

June went on, 'My boyfriend and I were in that restaurant. We were away over in the corner, so you didn't see us.'

Maureen avoided Sylvia's eye as she snapped at the junior, 'Kindly mind your own business! Be quick with washing those cups and hurry back to the desk.'

Sylvia spoke calmly. 'There's no need to get agitated, Maureen. I knew Lucas had taken you out for a meal.'

Maureen turned to face her. 'You did? Information from June, I suppose. The moment you stepped into the office she rushed with the news. I'll bet she was agog——'

'Wrong. I learnt of it last night. Lucas himself told me.'

Maureen's voice became cold. '*Last night?* Are you saying he left me—to go to *you*?'

'Certainly not.'

'He told me he was going to see his aunt.' Maureen frowned, then added. 'At least he said his aunt would be waiting for him.'

Sylvia smiled. 'But he didn't say *where* she'd be waiting? At the moment she's in my mother's number one bedroom.'

Maureen was bewildered. 'How can that be?'

'Mother has a convalescent home, but takes only three people.' Sylvia went on to explain how she had taken the birthday flowers to Amy Grayson and the state of her health when she had arrived. 'She was in dire need of help, so I took her home,' she finished.

June's eyes were full of admiration. 'Gosh, you're a fast worker!' she breathed.

'I'll say she is,' Karen agreed.

Sylvia sent sharp looks from one to the other. 'What's *fast worker* supposed to mean?' she demanded.

Karen grinned. 'We mean it was a smart move—one that would enable you to get closer to the boss.'

'It wasn't like that at all,' protested Sylvia.

Maureen's icy voice cut the silence that followed the denial. 'June is right. You're a fast worker, and a mighty cunning one as well.' She inhaled a deep breath to control any further accusations she had in mind. Instead she snapped, 'Come along, girls—back to work.' She swept from the room, the other two sidling after her.

Sylvia felt despondent as she returned to the computer. Her action in taking Amy Grayson home had not been with a view to closer relations with Lucas, but this, apparently, was what the staff thought. And if a naïve junior such as June could jump to this conclusion, it must also have been an obvious fact to Lucas. No wonder he had looked upon her action with suspicion!

The rest of the day passed without incident, and again she saw nothing of him. However, when she returned from her lunch break she discovered that the pile of papers on her table had increased, giving proof that he had been to her room during her absence. Proof, also, that he was avoiding her?

The question nagged at her until the necessity to concentrate forced her to brush it away. Yet it kept returning, and by the time the day ended she was calling herself a fool for allowing her thoughts to wander in his direction. It had been easy enough to get him off her mind seven years ago, so why not now?

When she reached home Amy's voice called to her as she entered the hall. 'Is that you, Sylvia?'

She went to the door of the number one bedroom, where she found Amy sitting up in bed and looking a little brighter. The room was enhanced by the basket of carnations, which were still looking fresh, and as Sylvia went closer to examine them she realised how one event relied upon another. If she had not offered to deliver this floral arrangement of long-stemmed beauty, Amy would not be here.

The older woman watched her change the position of a flower. 'They're lasting well,' she remarked. 'Dear Lucas, he always remembers my birthday. Did he say he'd be coming to see me tonight?'

Sylvia adopted a casual air. 'I haven't seen him today. I think he's been busy with Maureen. Do you want to see him for a special reason? If so we could phone and ask him to come.'

'It's just that I feel I've monopolised this room for long enough. It's time I went home.'

'Where you'll have a relapse,' said Ruth from the doorway. 'You've only just completed your course of antibiotics and the weather report has promised another cold snap.'

'If I stay much longer I'll need more nightdresses—I only snatched up a few. And I really do feel I'm imposing when you have so much to do.'

Ruth brushed the protest aside. 'Nonsense! I have Wiki, my good helper who comes each day during the week. Besides, you're doing an excellent job in keeping Mr Mackenzie entertained. He enjoys his chats with you.'

Amy giggled. 'You're the one he has his eye on!'

'Then I'd be glad if you'd stay and protect me,' Ruth returned with a laugh as she left the room.

Amy looked at Sylvia. 'I can't help wondering if Lucas has given thought to my suggestion.'

'Oh?' Sylvia guessed what she meant but did not care to admit it. It was not a subject she wished to discuss.

Amy went on, 'I mean about a partnership with Maureen.'

Sylvia found the thought most depressing. 'You really consider it would be a good idea?'

'Of course. The more I think about it, the better I like it. They've worked well together for years.'

'Is an alliance at work all he needs—or are you hoping it would develop into something more?'

'My dear, I'm not thinking of Maureen as a *wife* for Lucas. I'm merely considering her as a business partner.' Amy paused thoughtfully, then added, 'Still, after a while, one never knows what could happen.'

Sylvia's spirits had fallen. 'That's right—one never knows.'

Amy sighed. 'Sometimes I wonder if he'll ever marry. He's taking a long time to get over that girl.'

Sylvia was startled. 'Wh-what girl?'

'The one he was in love with years ago. I can tell you he was in such a state his grandfather and I were really worried about him.'

'You—met her, I suppose?'

'Never set eyes on her. Just as well, perhaps, or Grandfather might have throttled her!'

Sylvia swallowed but said nothing.

'We both knew he needed something else to think about,' Amy went on. 'His grandfather declared he knew the answer, and I well remember the day when he gave Lucas a sum of money and told him to build himself a castle. After that it was his serious mind that enabled him to concentrate on the best investments.'

Sylvia licked dry lips. 'Didn't he ever tell you a—a little—about this girl?'

'Only that she'd just turned seventeen and wasn't long out of a fairly strict boarding school. I tried to explain that there lay the answer. She was too young. She was only on the threshold of life. I longed to tell him that he probably bored her to tears, but that would have only added further hurt to his already injured pride.'

Sylvia kept her mouth tightly shut lest she told Amy how right she had been. But not any more. Lucas Carville no longer bored her to tears. In fact she had begun to suspect the situation had been reversed, and that *she* was the one who now bored *him* to distraction—apart from odd moments when it amused him to play with her emotions.

Lucas arrived later in the evening, and as Sylvia opened the door to him she knew that her pulses had quickened. She also knew that his eyes became hooded, taking in every inch of her appearance, and for a moment she regretted having changed into her turquoise leisure suit. The looseness of the soft trousers and top gave comfort, but did nothing to present a picture of enticing femininity.

He said, 'You look about—seventeen.'

The word jolted her memories, but she refused to attach any significance to it. 'Seventeen is a lovely age,' she declared, sending him a direct look. 'It would be nice to stay there.'

'How is my aunt?' Lucas demanded abruptly.

'She's been hoping you'd come to see her. She's now well enough to talk about going home, but Mother says it's a little too soon because she wouldn't stay in bed and could possibly suffer a relapse. Nor is there any need for her to leave here—unless you're about to command that she returns home,' she added after a thoughtful pause. 'Is that what you have in mind?'

'Of course not,' he gritted, his displeasure obvious. 'You must consider I'm a positive tyrant!'

'One never knows how people will react,' she replied quietly. 'Remember your annoyance when I brought her here.'

Lucas made no reply, and they walked in silence along the passage to the number one bedroom.

Amy's face beamed as he walked into the room. 'I knew you'd come, dear!' she exclaimed happily as he bent and kissed her.

Sylvia said, 'There'll be coffee in the living-room when you've finished talking with your aunt.'

'Thank you,' he said gravely, his eyes resting on her blonde hair. 'I presume Brookes is here as usual?'

She ignored his last words. 'Yes, he's in with his mother.'

Amy said, 'That poor woman is very fretful. Mr Mackenzie has chatted with her. He says she's anxious to know when I'll be leaving so that *she* can be moved into *this* room.'

'He's an old gossip!' exclaimed Sylvia, visualising Jock getting short shrift from Mrs Brookes. 'As for going home, I think you'll find the doctor will have the last say about that situation.'

Amy sighed. 'Yes, I suppose so. Besides, I'd be an extra worry for Lucas.' She turned to him anxiously. 'I'll need extra nighties. They're in my chest of drawers.'

'Right, I'll find them.'

'Now then, tell me about your day. Is Maureen coping with this—this different work you've given her?'

Maureen, Sylvia thought crossly. Amy Grayson is certainly well obsessed by the thought of *Maureen*! She looked at Lucas, wondering if he also shared these feelings, but the glint in the dark eyes returning her gaze betrayed nothing. Then as she left the room an imp forced her to smile at Amy and say, 'I'm sure he has plenty to tell you about Maureen.'

She bit her lip, and, feeling annoyed with herself for having uttered those words, she returned to the living-room, where she made an attempt to occupy herself until Lucas decided he'd spent sufficient time with his aunt. He would be with her for at least an hour, she felt sure, then found difficulty in concealing her surprise when he reappeared in less than half that period.

'I see you're all alone,' he remarked as he entered the room.

'Yes. Mother is with Mr Mackenzie, and Brian is still with his mother,' Sylvia explained.

'While you're waiting for him to emerge,' he taunted.

'Oh, no.' She smiled, refusing to rise to his bait. 'But I must say I'm surprised to see you leave Amy quite so soon.'

'I think she understands that I need to talk to you.'

'You do?' Her heart leapt with uncontrolled gladness. Was he about to ask her to reconsider her decision to leave his employment? And then instinct warned that this might not be what he had in mind. Cautiously she queried, 'What do you want to talk to me about?'

'Would it be possible to go somewhere private?' Lucas demanded.

'You mean to a place where we're unlikely to be interrupted?'

'Exactly.' There was a grimness in his tone.

She decided to ignore it, so she smiled and said, 'I'm becoming quite curious! We could walk to the bottom of the garden. When I was a small child I used to imagine there were fairies in the treetops at the end of the path.'

'At the moment I'm not interested in fairies. My concern is much more down to earth.'

'Oh? Well, our section backs on to the golf course. Mother often takes a convalescent for a walk beside the trees growing along its edge, but only when there are no golfers in sight, of course, because it would be dreadful if one happened to be struck by a stray ball.'

She found herself chatting nervously, her tension caused by the thought of going out into the moonlight with Lucas. At the same time she sensed a vague sternness in his attitude towards herself, and, wondering about it, she went to the laundry, where she found a woollen cape used by her mother when going outside on a cold day.

The concrete path beside the house led them past the number three bedroom where neither blind nor curtains had been drawn. The brightness of the lighted window drew Sylvia's gaze into the room, where Brian's mother lay propped against pillows while he sat beside her.

In that instant he turned and saw them pass. His sandy brows drew together in a scowl, and, springing to his feet, he crossed the room to fling open the window. 'Going for a walk?' he demanded.

Lucas stood still, then turned to grin at him. 'Only to find fairies at the bottom of the garden.'

'I've been sitting for hours. I could do with a walk.'

'Then take one, old boy—but not with us. We have private matters to discuss,' Lucas added, taking Sylvia's arm to lead her from the path and across the back lawn towards the trees bordering the end of Ruth's half-acre section of land.

The feel of his hand on her arm made her flesh quiver, but she gave no sign of it as they turned along the track running beside the edge of the golf course. Is this really happening? she wondered. Am I actually out in the moonlight with Lucas? Anticipation began to rise, causing her to feel sure that at any moment he would ask her to reconsider giving up her job at the office.

CHAPTER SIX

SYLVIA was conscious of an inner satisfaction that sent her spirits aloft. She stood still to gaze about her, drinking in the beauty of a landscape made mysterious by the moon which cast shadows across fairways, bunkers and greens. Beyond the course lay the hills of the forestry reserve, parts of them shrouded in a haze of thermal steam that rose from the Whaka-rewa-rewa thermal valley.

Turning to look at Lucas, she found his eyes resting upon her, and suddenly she sensed a brooding sombreness about him. It made her realise that the shadows were not only on the golf course—they were also in his mind.

'So you have need to talk to me?' she queried, wondering what was to come.

'Yes. I'd like to know what you're trying to achieve.' His words had become clipped.

His meaning escaped her. 'Achieve? What do you mean?'

'I mean what's the big idea?'

Her jaw dropped slightly. '*Big idea*—what on earth are you talking about?'

'Surely you can guess,' he snapped.

They had walked a distance along the path and again she stood still to turn and face him. Shaking her head, she said, 'Sorry, I'm not with you. I'm completely clueless.'

'Is that a fact?'

She caught the hint of a sneer, and even in the moonlight she could see the hardness of his mouth, the expression on his face which told her that remaining in his employ was not the subject he had in mind. Disappointment sent her spirits plummeting as she snapped, 'I can see something is bugging you, but I'm afraid you'll have to be more explicit.'

'Right, I'll try to spell it out. It's this idea you've put into Amy's head. You've made a bullet for her to fire.'

Nonplussed, Sylvia stared at him in silence until, exasperated, she said, 'I'm afraid I'm still not with you.'

A deep sigh indicated his impatience. 'You know exactly what I mean. I'm talking about your suggestion to Amy that I take Maureen into partnership——'

'*My* suggestion?' she cut in. 'You've got to be joking!'

'I think not. This evening she said quite clearly that it was you who put the idea into her head.'

'Amy said that?' She felt astounded.

'Most definitely.'

'But I didn't!'

'You're calling my aunt a liar?' His voice had become icy.

'No, of course not. I mean, she's mistaken.' What was Amy playing at? she wondered, then added quickly, 'Can't you see what's happened? The fact that I'm leaving has put the idea into her head. She doesn't want to see you left without Maureen—I mean, someone who can do auditing——' Her words trailed away.

Lucas brushed Maureen's ability aside. 'It might interest you to learn that this evening's visit consisted of one long argument. Amy became quite upset.'

'Poor Amy, she was really looking forward to seeing you.' Her voice became filled with sympathy for the older woman.

'Only to hammer home this partnership idea, I think.'

Sylvia became impatient. 'For Pete's sake, Lucas, surely you can understand she only has your interests at heart. And I can only repeat that the idea has come to her because—because she knows I'm leaving——'

Sylvia held her breath, waiting for him to take the opening she had presented, the opportunity to suggest that she stayed in the job. She did not expect him to actually *plead* with her—oh no, Lucas would never plead with *anyone*—but at least he could indicate that he did not want to see her leave. However, he remained silent, and a deep despondency began to grow within her.

Within moments the atmosphere between them had become so tense she began to wonder why she should continue to walk along this track with him. Then, just as she was on the verge of turning and running towards home, his next words surprised her.

'I think there's need for closer discussion.'

'Closer——?' she queried.

'Yes. Over here should be suitable.'

She remained wordless as he drew her towards the darker shadows of some tall trees bordering the golf course, several of them being deodar cedars with branches spreading to droop only a short distance from the track.

Within this place of concealment he held her against him, his fingers entwined in her hair until her head was forced back at an angle which enabled his cheek to rest against her forehead, then slowly, his arms tightened about her.

Not wanting to break the spell, she leaned against him, her heart thudding. And then his voice came from above her head.

'Perhaps you're right. No doubt it's because you're leaving that Amy thinks I should do something about making Maureen's job more permanent.'

Because you're leaving. Sylvia brushed the sound of the words from her mind, yet made no reply while experiencing the sudden rush of contentment in the feel of his arms about her body.

His voice continued softly. 'It's so difficult to believe the idea could have come from Amy.'

'Well, it did. So why should it be difficult?'

'Because she's never really liked Maureen. And when she came up with the suggestion that it's time I was thinking of taking a wife, I was really staggered. That's when I blew my top and told her to mind her own damned business.'

Sylvia's eyes were wide in the darkness. 'But she didn't mean you should consider marrying Maureen—did she?'

'Who else? We were talking about Maureen, weren't we? And then the thought struck me that this idea was another one put into her head by you.'

'Oh, no!' The words left her lips like a cry of distress.

'You're sure about that?' Lucas's voice was tinged with suspicion.

'Of course I'm sure. It's the last thing I'd suggest—unless——'

'Yes? Unless what?' he drawled.

'Unless you discover yourself to be in love with her, of course.'

He laughed. 'That's hardly likely.'

'How can you be so sure?'

'Because I have myself well under control. Never again shall I allow myself to become besotted, as I once was——'

'I doubt that you've ever been besotted over anyone. It was only your ego that suffered...' The words faded to a whisper as Sylvia recalled what Amy had said. He was in such a state his grandfather and I were really worried about him, she'd declared.

And then a mixture of sympathy and guilt, coupled with something she was unable to control, caused her to raise her face to brush his lips with her own. 'I'm sorry for having hurt you to that extent,' she said in a low voice.

'Then kiss me again to prove it.'

The words came in a tense command and she lifted her face without hesitation. His arms tightened about her, and as he drew her closer his hands manipulated her against the length of his body. Their pressure on her shoulderblades crushed her breasts against his chest, then a deft movement flicked his jacket open, causing her hardened nipples to be thrust against the soft material of his shirt.

Gently, his thighs moved against her with a potency that fanned inner embers to leaping flames, and as his kiss deepened her arms wound about his neck in a gesture of submission.

'Sylvia——' he murmured huskily.

She began to tremble while his mouth left her lips to follow the line of her jaw, and there they paused to nuzzle the lobe of her ear. A hand held her breast, the pad of his thumb caressing her nipple until a small moan of ecstasy escaped her. It was the first time she had heard herself utter such a sigh of delight, and with it she also heard the call of common sense.

Shakily, she said, 'Lucas, we must come down to earth.'

'Don't you know I'm making up for lost time? Surely you know what you do to me?' The words were murmured in her ear.

She was more than aware of his arousal, but she managed to keep her voice calm. 'We must keep our feet on the ground.'

Even as she spoke her mind flashed back to her thoughts of yesterday morning when she had wondered just how much depth of meaning his kisses contained. The memory caused warning bells to clang as she realised that this was part of his scheme.

Again she suspected he would make a bid for her affections, and when he felt sure she was nicely in love with him he would reject her—just as she had rejected him seven years ago. The tables would have been turned. Then, hugging his revenge, he would sit in his castle and gloat, no doubt with Maureen beside him.

She then recalled the decision she'd made, even going to the extent of raising her right hand as she had spoken the words aloud. Short shrift was what she had intended to give him. *Short shrift?* So what was she doing about it? Dared she ask? Dared she examine her own weakness of basking in the joy of being held against him? What was wrong with her?

Why was she unable to struggle against the pleasant tingles that filled her body with desire? *Desire.* She was almost trembling with a deep yearning to be much closer, for an intimate relationship—and *that*, she realised again, was exactly what Lucas had intended.

The knowledge was enough to stir her anger, and although she longed to shrug herself free of his embrace and race along the track she controlled the impulse. Instead she said, 'I think we should go home.'

He stared down into her face, his features barely discernible in the gloom cast by the overhead branches. 'You're becoming—bored?'

'Not exactly.'

'Afraid?'

'A little.' The admission came reluctantly.

His hands gripped her shoulders, shaking her slightly. 'Are you saying you're actually afraid of me—that you fear I'll take advantage of you?'

'Not in the way you mean.'

'Well, I'm glad you don't imagine you're about to be raped—although you must know that I want you,' he added bluntly. 'So what do you mean?'

Sylvia could feel the intentness of his gaze, but being unable to voice the words in her mind she remained silent.

But he was not to be put off. 'Come on, out with it. You know I wouldn't hurt you.'

'Wouldn't you?' Her tone had become bleak. 'I'm not so sure about that. I believe it's what you have in mind.'

He stared at her through the gloom. 'I really can't work out what it is you're trying to say.'

She took a deep breath, then decided to be honest. 'I mean that just as I hurt you, you are now trying to hurt me. Your aim is to—to get me into a state of loving you, and as soon as you're sure I'm longing for you to ask me to marry you, you'll stride off into the distance.'

A laugh escaped him.

She ignored it as she went on, 'That's what these kisses are all about—along with the ones on the track below the Buried Village. Nothing more, nothing less.'

Lucas's voice came with grating harshness, indicating that he had ceased to be amused. 'You're accusing me of being a devious, two-faced rotter—the love-you-and-leave-you type.'

Sylvia made no reply.

'At least one point is only too true. I do want to make love with you. That shouldn't be difficult to believe.'

'Not at all difficult,' she agreed crisply. 'But it's only because of your male needs, not because you have any love for me.'

'I had no idea you considered me to be such a cold fish,' he rasped. 'Is this how you thought of me seven years ago?'

She gave a sigh of utter weariness, then spoke rapidly, her voice low. 'Haven't I tried to explain? Do I have to spell it out again? At that time I was only seventeen and just out of school. I wasn't ready for commitment.'

'Yes, so you told me.'

'But could you understand that situation? No, you could not. All you could see was your own disappointment at being unable to tie me to your side.'

'I'll admit I was obsessed by you——' he began.

'Oh, yes, you admit that you were *then*, but you're *not now*,' she hissed accusingly. 'Really, Lucas, one would have thought you'd have matured beyond petty revenge!'

His voice came mockingly. 'I had no idea you'd be so astute at working things out—I mean at reading my devious mind.'

'I trust I'm not a complete nitwit, even if I don't happen to be as brilliant as Maureen——' She stopped, furious with herself.

'Ah, the thought of my closer association with Maureen bugs you?'

'Not at all,' she declared loftily.

'But she's on your mind, otherwise her name wouldn't have slipped from your tongue. Interesting. Most interesting,' he mused.

'Is it indeed? Now may we go home?' Sylvia moved to leave the shelter of the branches and return to the track, but his hand on her arm detained her.

Drawing her back into the gloom, he said, 'Just a minute. I've listened to your allegations with infinite patience, and now I'm curious to learn the answers to a couple of questions.'

'Oh?' She looked at him wonderingly.

'Have you ever been serious about a man?'

'No.' Better to be honest about it, she decided.

'You're twenty-four and have had plenty of time to become involved or to get married, yet there appears to be nobody in sight, apart from Brookes. I'd like to know why such a situation exists.'

'Really, this isn't your concern, Lucas,' she said coldly.

'I consider you owe me an answer—or shall I give you the answer?'

She laughed. 'OK, you tell me.'

'It's because you've never wiped me completely from your mind.'

'Nonsense,' she snapped haughtily. Yet his words startled her, because they were true. She had never forgotten Lucas. Over the years he had lingered in the back of her mind, lurking like a ghost that refused to be laid to rest.

He pursued relentlessly, 'No doubt other men have come along—plenty of them, because you're a very beautiful girl—but you've always retained a place for me right next to your heart.'

Sylvia forced a laugh. 'Your colossal ego is something to leave one staggered!'

'In fact I'm willing to bet you're still a virgin.'

'Mind your own damned business!' she hissed furiously.

'Ah, I thought so.' Lucas's voice rang with satisfaction. 'And that brings me to the second question.'

'Second?' Again she was startled. What more was there to come?

'It concerns your reaction to my embrace. Did you push me away or smack me over the ear? No, you did not,' he jeered.

She swallowed, but could find no words to refute the accusation.

'And why? Because you were longing to be held close to me.' His voice went on relentlessly. 'Don't you realise that your clinging arms, your lips parted to my kisses, have given you away?'

An angry gasp escaped her. 'I'll not listen to another word!' But even as she turned to leave him another sound made her freeze to the spot, then she caught her breath as she realised its source.

It was the air of a popular tune being whistled by a person who walked along the track, and as they peered cautiously through the branches they saw the figure of the tall man whose fair hair was illuminated by the moonlight.

'It's Brookes,' remarked Lucas with a chuckle as Brian passed their place of concealment.

'I can see that for myself,' Sylvia retorted crossly. 'Where can he be going?'

'Where else but to search for you?' Lucas murmured. 'Shall I give him a call?'

'Certainly not!' she gasped.

'Wouldn't you like him to join us beneath this tree? There's an old song—something about *Under the Deodar*. We could all sing it together.'

'You're quite mad!'

'Or don't you want him to know you're here alone with me?'

'I couldn't care less,' she shrugged.

'The deodar is an interesting cedar,' Lucas mused. 'Its home is the Himalayan foothills, where the Indians look upon it as sacred and a symbol of fruitfulness and durability.'

Sylvia's laugh rang with scorn. '*Durability*, you say? Huh! So what are *we* doing beneath its branches?' And with that parting shot she ran along the path towards home.

His long strides enabled him to catch her within seconds while his hand on her arm pulled her to a halt. Swinging her round to face him, he gritted, 'Not so fast! Do you want questions asked when you rush into the house looking as if you've just been electrocuted—face red, eyes glaring, hair standing on end?'

She snatched her arm from his grasp. 'I shan't look like that,' she declared haughtily, her chin lifted several inches higher.

'Then you'd be wise to simmer down right smartly.' His grin showed in the moonlight as he added, 'And don't raise your chin at me in that hoity-toity fashion. It's liable to be kissed.'

'You're—you're insufferable!'

'And you're making much ado about nothing,' he told her.

'*Nothing?* You can say it's *nothing*?' she flared bitterly. 'Leading me on to make me imagine I mean something to you is a fine joke, I suppose. Quite hilarious, in fact. Oh, yes, I understand. *Perfectly*.'

'What exactly do you understand *perfectly*?' he mocked.

'That you're merely getting your own back, of course. This is what you imagine I did to you. Please don't make me try to explain it again,' she pleaded wearily.

'The subject is closed?'

'Definitely closed. I shan't speak of it again.'

'Not even to hear any denials on my part?'

Her heart leapt. Was he about to refute her accusations? She gave him a few seconds to do so, but when he remained silent she said, 'They'd be difficult to believe.'

'So why try to convince you?'

They walked the rest of the distance in silence until they reached the back lawn, where Lucas paused and said, 'It's unfortunate that your head is filled with these negative thoughts. However, I'm unable to do very much about them.'

She looked at him mutely, longing to hear him say she was wrong, absolutely wrong, but no such assurance passed his lips.

Instead he said, 'I can only hope these mental agitations don't make your last days in the office too unhappy.'

'There's no need to be sarcastic!'

He frowned as though considering a question. 'Tell me again, why are you leaving? I can't remember the exact reason for terminating your job with me.'

Frustrated, Sylvia spoke through tight lips. 'Then let me refresh your memory. It's because you were satisfied I'd *come to heel*. Now that you've attained success you were sure I'd deliberately sought a job in your office for the sole purpose of renewing our previous acquaintance. You didn't actually *say* I'm a gold-digger, but the suspicion was sticking out of both ears.' Voicing the words almost made her shake with fury.

'So that was it?' he drawled. 'Strangely, I'd got it into my head that you were really running back to Brian.'

'Obviously there's no accounting for what goes into your head—and you know very well that my reason for returning to the estate agency office concerns Mother, rather than myself.'

He gave a slight shrug. 'No doubt her affairs give you as good an excuse as any other.'

As they entered the living-room Ruth's voice called from the kitchen, 'Is that you, Sylvia dear? Did you have a pleasant walk?'

'Very, thank you,' she replied without looking at Lucas.

Ruth said, 'I've made coffee for some and Horlicks for others. I'm sure Lucas would enjoy a hot drink.'

'Thank you,' he responded gratefully.

Ruth came into the room carrying a small tray. Smiling at him, she said, 'Would you like to take this to your aunt?'

He relieved her of the tray. 'Yes, I'd like a few more words with her before I leave.'

About Maureen? Sylvia wondered, then became aware of her mother making a request.

'You can take a tray to Mrs Brookes, dear. She's complained that she's hardly seen you since she arrived, and has even hinted that you might be avoiding her.'

Sylvia took the tray reluctantly. There was no need to admit that her avoidance of Ellen Brookes had been deliberate, and as she entered the number three bedroom the woman in the bed looked at her reproachfully. However, this was not unexpected.

Ellen Brookes was a thin, neurotic woman with a small face from which grey eyes seemed to look upon the entire world with reproach. It was almost as if she considered that most people owed her something, and now the sight of Sylvia forced a deep sigh from her.

'So, you've seen fit to come and see me at last!'

Sylvia put on a bright smile. 'How are you, Mrs Brookes? Feeling much better, I hope.'

'No, I'm not. My bruises are *terrible*. My ribs are so *painful*!' She went on to describe how she had fallen over the vacuum cleaner, and how she had to do her own housework because help in the home was so unreliable. They didn't get into the *corners*, nor could they be *trusted* with precious possessions. The tirade ceased as she demanded abruptly, 'Where's my son?'

Sylvia was taken aback. 'Brian?'

'Of course. Who else?' The question was snapped impatiently. 'He was good enough to go out searching for you.'

'May I ask why?' Sylvia's tone had become cool.

'Because he wanted to make sure you were quite *safe* with—with that Carville man.'

'His concern was thoroughly unnecessary,' Sylvia replied stiffly, annoyed by the other's insinuation.

'Nevertheless Brian is very concerned for you—but of course you've always known *that*.'

'Is your Horlicks satisfactory, Mrs Brookes? Nice and hot, I hope?' Sylvia asked, making an attempt to veer away from the subject of Brian while edging towards the door.

Ellen Brookes saw the movement. 'Please don't go away,' she said sharply. 'It's time we had a talk.' She took several sips of her Horlicks, nodded approval, then said, 'I must say it really annoys me to see a girl make my son so unhappy.'

Sylvia ignored the fact that the girl referred to was herself. 'I doubt if he's unhappy, Mrs Brookes,' she returned calmly. 'Besides, I'm sure Brian can take care of himself.'

'No, he can't,' the fond mother snapped. 'He needs a good wife to do things for him. I'm afraid I'll not be at his side forever. This fall has made me feel so *old*!' she finished plaintively.

Sylvia made an effort to comfort her. 'You worry about him too much. He's a grown man.'

'Of course I worry—I'm his mother, aren't I? You wait until you have a son. He'll always be your little boy whatever his age.' Suddenly she became distressed. 'And now Brian has gone outside in the night air without his jacket. He might catch a chill,' she almost wailed.

Sylvia recalled seeing Brian through the window. 'I'm sure he's wearing a jersey. He'll be all right.'

'He needs a jacket as well,' Ellen Brookes persisted. 'It's on the chair—and as he's out searching for you I consider you should take it and see if you can find him.' The words, spoken imperiously, were issued in the form of an order.

A small laugh escaped Sylvia. 'Surely you must be joking?'

Ellen Brookes sent her a stony stare. 'Indeed I am not. Would I joke about my son's welfare? Furthermore, I consider it to be your duty to take his jacket to him.'

Sylvia made an effort to keep her patience, then took a deep breath as she said, 'I'm sorry, Mrs Brookes, the thought of going out to search for Brian appals me. I'm afraid he'll have to take care of himself.'

'You're saying you refuse to go?'

'That's right. I haven't the slightest intention of doing so.'

'And this man Lucas Carville. Would you also refuse to take a jacket to him?' The question came in a dry tone.

Sylvia smiled sweetly. 'I doubt if he'd be harmed by a little night air.'

Another sigh escaped the woman in the bed. 'Well, at least I know one person who would take Brian's jacket to him.'

'Is that so?' Sylvia was curious, despite herself.

'Maureen—his friend who also works in the Carville office—she'd have gone at once.'

Sylvia doubted this statement, but was unable to resist saying, 'Then it's a pity she's not here to do so.'

'Maureen's a lovely girl—and so clever.'

'Very efficient indeed,' Sylvia agreed.

'I know she likes Brian, and I think he admires her. A mother can usually tell these things.'

Sylvia watched her narrowly. Was Mrs Brookes trying to make her jealous? And then she decided that this was another statement to be doubted. It was just Ellen Brookes being Brian's mother.

Then the latter surpassed herself by stating firmly, 'Of course, any mother will tell you that *no* girl is good enough for her son.'

Sylvia felt she'd had enough, yet she was unable to suppress a laugh as she said, 'Mrs Brookes, that attitude is the surest way to frighten away any potential daughter-in-law!'

Brian spoke from the doorway. 'What attitude is this?'

Sylvia turned to face him. 'I'm sure your mother will explain.'

But apparently he was not in the mood to listen to any explanation his mother could offer. Instead he stared at Sylvia. 'Where were you? I've been out looking for you.'

'So I've been told.'

'I went through the gate at the bottom of the garden, and after going a distance in one direction I turned and went back the other way. There wasn't a sign of you.'

Sylvia decided to be frank. 'We were standing beneath one of the trees along the edge of the golf course. We watched you go past.'

An expression of anger crossed Brian's face. 'Why didn't you let me know you were there?'

'Because we had private matters to discuss,' she told him, keeping her tone calm only with an effort.

A rapid glance shot from mother to son, then Brian frowned. 'Private matters? Wouldn't the office be a more appropriate place, rather than the dark shadows of a tree?'

Sylvia smiled at him. 'Didn't I say these were *private* affairs? The office is for business matters.' She paused, taking in the disapproval on Ellen Brookes's face and the belligerence on Brian's features. She longed to shout angrily that her movements were not their concern, but she forced her voice to remain steady as she spoke to Brian. 'Your walk will have made you thirsty. I'll pour coffee for you. It'll be in the living-room.'

She left them, feeling positive they would begin talking about her at once, but this irritation disappeared when she found that Lucas had returned to the living-room, where he sat talking to Ruth.

Surprised to see him, she said, 'I thought you'd still be with Amy.'

'She was drowsy,' he explained. 'She drank her Horlicks quickly, then seemed to have little wish to talk.'

The look he sent her appeared to say much more, causing her to wonder if the subject of Maureen had come up, but her thoughts were interrupted as Brian came into the room.

He was smiling broadly as he went to Sylvia and gave her an unexpected hug. 'Thank you, darling—that was very sweet of you,' he beamed.

Taken aback, she went scarlet as she shrugged him away. 'What are you talking about?' she demanded angrily.

'Mother told me what you were about to do.'

She could only gape at him.

He went on, 'She said you realised I'd gone out into the cool night air without my jacket and that you feared I might catch a chill.'

Sylvia could hardly believe the words she was hearing. 'Your mother actually said—*that*?'

'She told me that just as I walked into the room you'd been on the verge of rushing out to search for me—with my jacket, of course.'

It was almost impossible to control her fury, and then the laugh that escaped Lucas made her swing round to glare at him. As she expected, his eyes were full of mockery, while the expression on his face made her squirm with inward rage. It was obvious he believed every word Brian had uttered, and the knowledge caused a surge of defiance to rear its head.

Turning to Brian, she said with forced sweetness, 'It's still only September and the spring air can be cold. I'd hate to see you struck down with pneumonia.'

'A most sensible attitude to take,' Lucas agreed smoothly, obviously having more difficulty in concealing his mirth. Then he turned to Brian, his tone sardonic. 'How are you feeling, old chap? Not poorly, I trust.'

Sylvia looked at Lucas reproachfully, realising he was not really laughing at Brian. His amusement was directed towards herself, because here was proof that her concern for Brian was strong enough to send her outside alone to search for him in the moonlight. OK, so let him think as he wished. After all, why should she care?

CHAPTER SEVEN

THE question continued to nag at her. Indeed, why should she care?

During the next few days it continued to squirm in her mind, rearing its head at the most unexpected moments, and, although pushed aside by the necessity to concentrate at the computer, it persisted in returning. Nor was she able to find an answer.

The next day she saw little of Lucas apart from one occasion when he stopped at her door. She expected to be handed more work, but instead he spoke in a manner that was full of mock anxiety.

'No doubt you've spoken to Brookes this morning?'

Surprised, she raised her brows. 'No. Why do you ask?'

'Surely you've phoned to make sure he hasn't started sneezing?'

'You must be out of your mind!' she snapped.

'The night air is so dangerous,' he teased. 'Especially without a jacket.'

The remark gave Sylvia the opening she needed. 'I'll have you know I had no intention of rushing out with his jacket. The idea was his mother's entirely.'

'Well, don't tell Brian—he'd be so disappointed. However, I'm glad you told me. It renews my faith in your common sense. Besides, how many kisses can a girl take in one evening?'

The hardness in his tone did not escape Sylvia, but before she could snap back a suitable reply he had departed for his office. So he was sure there'd have been kisses in the moonlight between herself and Brian. Drat the man and his suppositions! And drat Brian for putting her in this situation. But once again, why allow it to get under her skin?

Thursday was a similar day, and when Lucas appeared to have little or no desire to linger in her room Sylvia was almost grateful to be able to pass on a message concerning his aunt. She went to his room and knocked on the door, then noticed that her entry caused his face to become an expressionless mask.

'Yes? You have a problem?'

'No. It's just about Amy. Mother and the doctor have agreed she's well enough to go home this coming Sunday, and Amy asked me to remind you to get food in before the weekend.'

'She's decided I'll not be visiting her before then?'

Sylvia hesitated. 'I think she feels you're annoyed with her. Are you annoyed with her?' she felt compelled to ask.

'Amy must learn not to meddle in my business—and more especially in my emotional affairs,' Lucas stated coolly.

'She looks upon you as a son,' Sylvia reminded him gently. 'Your mother's sister, remember?'

He said nothing.

'And she also thinks you'll be too busy to visit her this evening. Also, as tomorrow is Friday, she wanted to make sure you have meat in the house.'

He laughed. 'The day I starve will be the day!'

'Well, I've delivered the message.' Then, fearing a taunt about Brian might spring to his mind, Sylvia hurried back to the computer.

The next morning seemed to bring depression, perhaps because it was Friday. It meant she had only one more week of work in Lucas Carville's offices, which also meant that next Friday would be her last day of association with him. And again she asked herself why this should concern her.

As usual she saw little of him. In fact she saw little of any of the staff until the afternoon tea-break when they congregated in the kitchen at three o'clock.

It became obvious that Maureen was in a happy mood, but the reason for it did not become clear until they were about to return to their respective tasks. Then, almost as if unable to keep the matter to herself, she said, 'I'll be leaving work as soon as possible this evening. I'll need to fix my hair. Actually, Lucas said I could leave a little early.'

Karen looked interested as she said, 'That sounds as if you're going out on an interesting date.'

Maureen looked smug. 'You can put a ring round that particular statement!'

They waited in silence to hear more, but Maureen did not enlighten them. Instead she slid a side glance at Sylvia which almost shouted *wouldn't you like to know*?

But Sylvia did not need to be told. Maureen, she felt sure, was being taken out by Lucas. Hadn't he said she could leave a little earlier than usual? Thinking about it, she was assailed by a sudden stab of jealousy. Was he following his aunt's advice after all? Was it the beginning of a closer relationship between them?

She returned to the computer with further depression settling upon her, and she was almost ready to finish for the day when Lucas walked into the room. She knew he had had a busy day, but in some mysterious way he managed to look as virile and as fresh as he had at nine o'clock in the morning.

He glanced at the work that had come off the machine. 'You've been busy—really flat out for most of the day.'

'Yes.' She looked at him wonderingly, sensing there was more to come, because Lucas seldom came into her room without a reason. And then his next words really surprised her.

'Could you do with a little relaxation after a hard day's work?'

'It would be pleasant,' she admitted warily, wondering what he meant, because it was unlike Lucas to ask vague questions.

'Or perhaps you have a prior engagement for this evening?'

'No—although I understand you yourself have plans.'

Surprise flickered in the dark eyes. 'Yes, I have plans, but as yet I haven't mentioned them.'

'Oh, well—Maureen said you'd given her permission to go home early to do her hair.'

'Which made you presume I was taking her out?'

'I'll admit it did sound like it. Not that it's my concern, of course,' Sylvia added hastily.

'Actually, my plan was to ask you to have dinner with me this evening,' Lucas told her.

She looked at him in silence, hardly able to believe her ears.

He went on, 'When Maureen told me she was being taken out to dinner I thought it would be nice to do likewise. So shall we make it a date?'

She controlled the excitement rising within her. 'Yes, thank you, it would be pleasant,' she said as casually as possible.

'Right. I'll call for you at seven o'clock.' Then he left her abruptly, leaving her to wonder whether the invitation had been real or her imagination.

She hurried home with a swirl of thoughts twisting about in her head. Lucas Carville was actually taking her to dinner! He wasn't taking Maureen as she had presumed—he was taking her, and she must be ready on time. So—first a shower, then her hair in hot rollers, and then the problem of what to wear.

Yet in truth this was no problem, because she had recently purchased a deep violet dress cut on the latest sophisticated lines. It contrasted with her blonde hair and made her eyes look like purple pools, although its low neckline had brought mutterings of *cleavage* from Ruth. Was it too formal? she wondered. No, better to be overdressed than underdressed. Besides, she was going out with Lucas. She must look her best.

When she was ready she went into the number one bedroom where he was spending a short time with his aunt. He stood up as she walked in, his eyes holding undisguised admiration. 'There'll be wolf whistles from all sides,' he commented.

She flushed, pleased by his praise, then turned to Amy. 'You've had a comfortable day?'

'Yes. I've been up and walking about. I made the mistake of visiting that woman in number three. My goodness, her son must be an absolute paragon!' She paused to examine Sylvia's dress. 'I must say you look very nice, my dear.'

Despite the compliment, Sylvia thought the older woman's expression had become veiled. There had been no suggestion of her being pleased to see them go out together, she noticed, so was Amy *displeased* about it? Did she consider Lucas should be escorting Maureen rather than herself?

This sudden suspicion had the effect of dampening Sylvia's inner glow of happy anticipation, but she resolved it would not be allowed to spoil her evening. Nevertheless, she found difficulty in making cheerful conversation.

Lucas noticed her silence, and as they drove along Fenton Street towards the city he sent her a side glance. 'You're very quiet.'

Impulse caused her to say, 'I have a strong suspicion that Amy considers you should be taking out—somebody else.'

He stared straight ahead. 'I was hoping you'd miss that subtle message. It was aimed at me, rather than at you. When Amy sets her mind on a project she goes about it in a peculiar manner.'

'I don't understand.'

'Then forget it. Just concentrate on having a pleasant evening. You haven't asked where I'm taking you.'

Sylvia forced herself to join his lighter mood. 'I'm looking on it as a mystery trip. I'll know where we're going when we get there.'

'Can't you guess? The last time I took you there was seven years ago. You'd scarcely stepped out of nappies—or so I've been led to believe.'

'But we're going in the wrong direction for Waiotapu.'

'Was that the only place we went to?'

She blinked, making an effort to remember other places they had visited so long ago. Yet suddenly it seemed as if it had been only yesterday. 'We're going to Aorangi Peak,' she said quietly and with perception. 'Is this to be another nostalgic trip?'

'Only if you wish to make it so,' Lucas returned nonchalantly.

The slight shrug accompanying his words told her it had been a mistake to ask that last question, and to keep the mood light she said, 'Aorangi Peak is a most suitable name for a restaurant situated on a mountain. It means clouds in the sky.'

'You're well versed in Maori words?'

'Not at all. I usually ask Wiki. She speaks fluent Maori and is looked on as an authority on their culture.'

They had driven through the city and had reached the outskirts when he slowed to turn left along Mountain Road. After a flat stretch it twisted uphill to the heights of Mount Ngongotaha where the restaurant was situated.

'Has Wiki told you what Ngongotaha means?' he asked.

'Yes. She pronounces it Nor-nor-ta-ha. She said *ngongo* means to drink, and that a *taha* is a calabash. According to Maori legend Ihenga went up this mountain and met a fairy woman who offered him a drink from her calabash. However, he became afraid and ran away.' She paused, then added smoothly, 'Some men do.'

Lucas frowned. 'Do what?'

'Run away. I mean, they're not very persistent.'

He ignored the subtle reference to seven years ago by saying, 'Who the devil was Ihenga?'

'Wiki says he was the first man to come inland from the coast. More than six hundred years ago he pushed his way through dense bush and undergrowth to discover hot pools and lakes. He named the place Rotorua. *Roto* is the word for lake, while *rua* means it was the second one he discovered.'

He said, 'I suppose most of the local people know these stories, but I'm afraid I've been too busy to catch up on them.'

'That's understandable. However, anything you want to know, just ask Wiki.' Speaking of the legends had enabled her to feel more relaxed, perhaps because they helped to clear her mind of more personal matters.

When they reached the restaurant Lucas parked the car, then led her into what was known as Ihenga's Lookout cocktail lounge, and while Sylvia knew the view from this altitude was extensive she barely glanced at it. Instead her attention was focused on Lucas whose handsome appearance stamped him as being a sophisticated man of the world.

He handed her a sherry, then said, 'A pity this place couldn't have been here when Ihenga arrived. I doubt that he'd have turned and fled—especially with a fairy such as yourself about the place. I suppose you know you look absolutely stunning.'

She flushed at the compliment. 'Thank you, kind sir.' She held back the urge to tell him he was the most devastating man in the lounge, and that his perfectly fitting dark blue suit did nothing to conceal his athletic virility.

But of course this was impossible, because he might imagine she had a purpose in view—although what purpose he thought she could have escaped her entirely, unless he expected her to admit she had no wish to leave his employment. Was he waiting for her to plead to be kept on? Did he really think she'd climb down to that extent? *No way.* Her pride simply wouldn't allow it.

Almost as though reading her thoughts Lucas leaned back in his chair and drawled lazily, 'Am I right in assuming you have only one more week with us? The time has flown and I've been too busy to keep up with events.'

Here it comes, she thought. He's giving me the opportunity to say I don't want to leave. But although she sought for the words she was unable to utter them, and instead she said, 'Yes, one more week, and that will pass quickly.'

He looked at her unsmilingly. 'I've appreciated your work on the computer. You've been most efficient.'

'I'm glad to have given satisfaction,' Sylvia said primly. 'I hope that whoever replaces me will also give satisfaction.'

'The people in the employment agency know exactly the type of person I need.' His tone was complacent.

She peeped at him from across the top of her glass. 'They slipped up where I was concerned, but then they weren't to know——'

'Yes? They weren't to know—what?'

'That you wouldn't have wanted to employ me.'

'If I hadn't wanted to employ you, I wouldn't have done so,' Lucas pointed out drily. 'And kindly remember that you are the one who has no further wish to work for *me*.' His expression became thoughtful. 'Was it your intention to take a quick look at what I've achieved before throwing the job back at me? That's what you've done.'

So he was tossing the ball back into her court. 'You know what brought *that* on,' she said, her voice tense with the longing to remind him of her reason for bringing about this situation. She waited for him to ask her to change her mind, but, as she had expected, she waited in vain.

'So be it,' he said, the slight lift of his shoulders indicating that the subject was closed.

Sylvia almost wept as she realised things were going wrong. *Damn* this conversation! she fumed inwardly. It's ruining the evening. First there had been Amy's attitude, and now *this*. Turning to Lucas, she said, 'As a matter of curiosity, why did you invite me out this evening? Is it to be a—a farewell gesture? If so it could have waited until next Friday.'

'Is it not possible for me to want to take you out *this* Friday?'

She frowned. 'I suppose so—yet I can't help feeling you had something more than a mere wish on your mind.'

'Are you suggesting there was an ulterior motive behind the invitation?' His tone held amusement.

'Perhaps something prompted the wish. Sooner or later the answer might show itself to me.'

'When it does, please let me know. It could be interesting.' He glanced at her empty glass. 'Another sherry?'

'No, thank you. I've already had two generous ones that have been potent enough to loosen my tongue—even to the extent of being ungracious enough to suspect your reason for bringing me here. I'm sorry about that.'

'Suspicions are often caused by inward niggles. Is something niggling at you?' Lucas asked innocently.

Sylvia controlled an almost overwhelming desire to scream *yes—yes*, something definitely niggles at me. Can't you see what it is?

He sat looking at her, his dark eyes trying to probe her mind, but as it was impossible for him to read her thoughts he said, 'Out with it. I can see you're troubled, deep down.'

'Am I so transparent?' she asked.

'Hasn't anyone ever told you that your face is—expressive?'

'Yes, I've been told, but it's not something I keep remembering.'

The reminder made her afraid to look at him—afraid that he might guess that she yearned for him to ask her to remain in her job. *Why didn't he do so?* And then the answer came clearly, hitting her with force and making her look the truth in the eye. Obviously he didn't want her to be there. It was as simple as that.

The knowledge caused a pain somewhere near the region of her heart, until common sense began to whisper urgently. Ignore it, stupid. You're in your best dress at Aorangi Peak. You're with Lucas—so just live for the moment. And having advised herself to this extent she turned to smile at him.

'That's better,' he drawled, his eyes resting on her lips. 'The clouds appear to have lifted, although you still haven't told me what niggled at you.'

Sylvia shook her head. 'Please, not another word about me. I'm a boring subject. But I notice you haven't said much about yourself.'

He grinned. 'I can begin by admitting I'm hungry! Let's go into the Mokoia Room, as they call the dining-room.'

His hand on her bare arm sent bubbles of excitement into her bloodstream, but she managed to appear calm as he led her across the thick, richly patterned carpet and into the restaurant. They were guided towards a table beside an expanse of glass which, apart from its supporting pillars, offered an unsurpassed vista of the surrounding land and water.

The view below them was breathtaking—a panorama spreading over the city's sparkling lights, across the lake to where Mokoia Island sat like a partly submerged mushroom, and to a distant glow in the sky where the rising moon outlined the silhouette of Mount Tarawera.

At last she dragged her eyes from it to study the menu, mentally tossing between marinated quail salad served with quail eggs and Cumberland sauce, or South Island salmon *flambé au Grand Marnier*. Looking up, she met Lucas's eyes across the top of the glossy page. 'Salmon, I think.'

'You don't fancy quail?'

'No, thank you. I often watch those little birds running across the lawn. I couldn't eat them.'

He studied the menu again. 'There's baked lamb fillet with fresh mint filling and raspberry vinegar sauce—or choice pan-fried venison backstraps served with morello cherry sauce.' Then, teasingly. 'As you're not watching lambs skip in the fields, or looking at deer in the bush, either of those dishes should be suitable.'

Sylvia remained unruffled. 'Nor am I watching salmon leap in the streams, which makes it equally suitable. Happy to be providing you with your little joke, sir,' she added sweetly.

The wine waiter at his side delayed further conversation, and as the man left the table she switched from the subject of food by turning towards his own interests. 'I've seen so little of you during the week. Everything is going well, I hope?'

'Yes. No major problems at the moment.'

Apparently her own pending departure was not being looked on as a problem, she noticed. 'Of course, if there were you have Maureen to help solve them,' she remarked.

'Maureen has been with me for years,' he reminded her gravely.

'I'm glad you have someone to help keep your castle intact.' The words were spoken flippantly.

'Actually, my castle has turned somewhat sour on me,' he told her.

The words surprised her. 'Oh? How could it do that?'

'By not giving me the return I expected.'

'You mean—financially?'

'It has nothing to do with money. I can only say that not all of Grandfather's promises concerning it have come true. If you must know the truth, I've lost interest in it.'

'That's only because you've attained your goal. It's the old story of it being better to travel hopefully than to arrive.'

'Quite the little philosopher, aren't you? However, at the moment my castle is sadly empty.'

Sylvia sent him an affable smile. 'Well, don't let it get you down. I'm sure Maureen will help you fill it——' The words died on her lips as she happened to glance across the room in time to see a couple being led to a nearby table. Keeping her voice low, she said, 'Would you believe that Maureen and Brian have just arrived?'

'Yes, I'd believe it. They've taken long enough to get here.'

Her eyes widened. 'You *knew* they were coming?'

'Maureen happened to mention it.' The words came casually.

Sylvia pondered the question darting about in her mind until at last she knew it had to be asked. The smile she sent across the table softened the suspicion in the query. 'Was this your purpose in bringing me here this evening? I mean, because you knew Brian and Maureen would be here?'

There was a silence while Lucas considered his reply. 'It could have had a bearing on it,' he admitted in an offhand manner.

'Is Maureen playing hard to get?' she teased, then knew the suggestion to be ridiculous because this man need only raise a finger and Maureen would come running. Nevertheless she added, 'Is it possible you're flaunting me at her?'

'You're being utterly daft!' he rasped angrily.

'Are you sure about that?' she asked in a soft voice.

'If you must know the truth, it's the other way round. I thought you'd be interested in seeing them together.'

'You're saying you wanted me to know Brian was taking Maureen out? But I told you, I know I'm not the only pebble on his particular beach.'

'Knowing is one thing, seeing is something different,' he shrugged.

'One would almost imagine you have my interests at heart!'

'Would that idea be so very far-fetched?'

'At least the answer has raised its head.'

He frowned. 'Your meaning escapes me. The answer to what?'

'To your purpose in bringing me here.'

'Oh, *that*. Believe me, it's only part of the answer.'

'I'm agog to learn the other part,' Sylvia said drily.

'The fact that I've wanted to take you out.'

She became conscious of a pleasant inner glow that caused her colour to deepen. 'Thank you. Those words make me feel much happier. That's if you mean them, of course.'

'I mean them,' he declared firmly. 'Let me prove them by taking you out again tomorrow. Let's go to Mokoia Island. I haven't been there for years.'

Further excitement grew within her. 'Neither have I. It would have to be on the two o'clock launch trip after my Saturday morning chores when I do a few odd jobs for Mother.'

'That'll suit me nicely.'

'You could come for lunch, and then you'll see Amy—unless——' She paused, her eyes clouding. 'Unless it'll upset her to learn that you're taking me out—*again*.'

'Nonsense. You don't know Amy as I know Amy.'

'Well, if you're sure.' Her spirits soared even higher as she turned to stare through the huge pane of plate glass, then directed soft words towards the island. 'We'll look forward to walking along your tracks tomorrow, Mokoia.'

Lucas followed her gaze to where the lone sentinel lay almost in the centre of Lake Rotorua. Despite the glow of moonlight it was hazily shrouded with a mysterious eeriness that not even its surrounding dappled waters could dispel.

Whimsically he queried, 'Do you think Tutanekai's ghost still walks there? Does he still play his flute to Hinemoa on the mainland?'

'Of course not. She sat on a rock listening to his love song, then swam across the lake to meet him, remember?'

'Not really. I wasn't there. It's about three hundred years ago.'

'One can't live in Rotorua without learning the story of Tutanekai and Hinemoa, and how she had had to swim because her father had tried to keep them apart. He'd ordered all canoes to be pulled high on the beach, so there was no other way to reach the man she loved——'

'A fortunate man, Tutanekai.' His tone dripped irony.

Sylvia allowed the pointed remark to pass over her head. 'When she reached Mokoia she lay and relaxed in a warm thermal pool. A short time later Tutanekai was led to her by his slave, who discovered her when he'd been sent to collect water——'

'Whereupon she was immediately swept up and carried off to bed.'

Sylvia ignored the interruption and all it implied. 'Today tourists splash in the pool,' she said.

'Have you swum in Hinemoa's pool?'

'Only many years ago, when I was a small child.' She paused for a few moments, then sent him an amused smile. 'So you see, their ghosts should be together on Mokoia, especially as they've always been known as New Zealand's most famous lovers. Wiki declares their descendants are still living in the district.'

Shadows fell across their table as Brian and Maureen arrived in time to hear Sylvia's last words. 'Don't believe everything Wiki says,' Brian advised in a jovial manner, then added, 'We thought we'd say hello while waiting for our food to be served.'

Lucas stood up. 'We were discussing Hinemoa and Tutanekai. Sylvia and I are taking a trip to the island tomorrow afternoon.'

Maureen gave a sigh of envy. Her eyes had taken in details of Sylvia's dress and turned to gaze up into Lucas's face. 'What a lovely idea! I haven't been to Mokoia for years.'

He stared at her thoughtfully, then said, 'If there's nothing to prevent Brian from taking you tomorrow we could make it a party of four—unless you yourself aren't free.'

'Oh, yes, I'm free.' Her face glowed as she turned to Brian. 'Please say we can go!'

Their words fell on Sylvia's ears like a deluge of icy water, swamping her with bitter disappointment. Her spirits plunged as she realised that Lucas had actually asked Brian and Maureen to join them on their trip to Mokoia. The afternoon was ruined before it had even begun. However, she forced a smile of agreement lest he sensed the deep despondency that had descended upon her.

Lucas turned to Brian. 'I suppose it's OK with you?'

A gleam appeared in the light blue eyes. 'Yes, I'd like that. Heaven alone knows when I last walked along those bush tracks—or when we last swam in Hinemoa's pool,' he added, turning to Sylvia.

His last words sent a shock of fury through her, but she remained calm. 'I've never swum in Hinemoa's pool with you. You're probably thinking of somebody else.'

'You can't possibly have forgotten,' Brian declared airily.

A wave of agitation swept her. 'No, Brian, we've *never* swum in that pool—at least, not together.'

'Come off it, Syl—your memory can't be that bad,' he drawled.

But Sylvia refused to allow his statement to pass unchallenged. She stood up and faced him, glaring at him angrily. 'Don't you *dare* persist in saying we've swum in Hinemoa's pool, *because we have not*!'

Maureen giggled. 'Shut up, the pair of you! You're making spectacles of yourselves!'

It was true. Other diners were turning to stare at the girl who had sprung to her feet, and, glancing about her, Sylvia realised that Maureen was right. She was making a fool of herself.

Then Lucas intervened by speaking in calm tones to Brian. 'We'll meet you at the two o'clock launch. Now, if you'll excuse us, I believe our meal is on its way across the room.'

They took the hint and left, Maureen walking with a slight sway of the hips that was probably meant to catch Lucas's attention.

'Sorry about that exhibition,' muttered Sylvia as she almost flopped back into her seat.

'It was—interesting.' His tone sounded flat.

'I'm glad you found it so. Personally, I found it revolting.' She picked up her knife and fork, then put them down again, feeling unable to eat. 'And why you found it necessary to ask them to join us tomorrow, I'll never know.'

'I can only repeat, it was interesting, especially that bit about swimming in Hinemoa's pool, which really intrigued me.'

Sylvia became alarmed. 'I trust you didn't believe that fool.'

'You do?'

'Brian's a lying hound!'

'Really?'

Her alarm turned to horror. She felt cold and even less able to eat, and as she watched him enjoy the food on his plate she said, 'I believe you think I'm a liar.'

'Then you'll have to convince me to the contrary.'

'Why should I bother? Are you likely to believe me? "Convince a man against his will, he's of the same opinion still,"' she quoted.

Lucas merely looked at her in silence.

She went on, 'I've already stated that I've never swum in that pool with Brian, and I can't say more than that. Nor am I able to see why any of this should be of interest to you.'

'It's just a matter of truth or untruth. I hate lies.'

'I can understand how you feel, because I also hate liars. They're despicable. They steal a person's faith. Daddy always declared a liar to be as bad as a thief. I feel distressed to know you've put me into that category.'

'Really, you're exaggerating. Nor have you touched your food.'

'You'd like to see it choke me? That's what it would do!' Sylvia snapped.

'You're feeling really miserable, huh?' His voice had softened while his eyes surveyed her with sympathy.

His unexpected compassion had an effect upon her, and to her utter humiliation her eyes filled. She dabbed at them furiously, using her table napkin, then spoke with a slight tremor in her voice. 'If you'll excuse me I'll—I'll phone for a taxi and go home.'

'That'll be over my dead body,' he gritted. 'I brought you here and I'll take you home, whether you like it or not.'

'I've no wish to remain with a man who considers me to be a liar!'

'For Pete's sake, forget it,' he urged.

'Nor have I any desire to go to Mokoia tomorrow. You've completely ruined all thoughts of that trip.'

'Now you listen to me, Sylvia Sinclair. First, you can snap out of this fit of the blues. Secondly, you can get it into your head that I do not look upon you as a liar.'

'You made it plain that you *do*,' she accused in a dull voice.

'Not plain at all. You *presumed* it was what I believed. Please give me credit for realising that Brian was trying to goad you. He was probably annoyed to find you here with me.'

She gaped at him. 'I hadn't thought of that.'

'And there's a third point. You will come to Mokoia as planned. A party of four has been arranged, and your petty irritations must not be allowed to spoil it for others.'

'*Petty?* Huh! I like that! Thank you very much. By *others* I suppose you mean Maureen. No doubt you'd prefer her company to mine.' The words came tumbling bitterly.

'Just as much as you'd prefer Brian's company to mine,' Lucas retorted, then grinned suddenly. 'Now please eat that food—and remember you have Pavlova topped with whipped cream and kiwi fruit to follow.'

Sylvia lifted her fork and began to eat, finding herself to be more in need of food than she had realised.

'That's better,' he approved, watching her.

After that there was silence between them until a question leapt into her mind, causing her to look at him curiously. 'Why did you invite them to join us?' She longed to add, *and spoil our day*.

His expression became inscrutable. 'Because I'd like to see them enjoy an outing together.'

'How very kind! What you're really saying is that you intend to watch Maureen's unguarded reaction to Brian's wiles and flattery,' Sylvia accused shrewdly. 'Lucas Carville, you're a devious devil!'

'Thank you for the compliment,' he returned gravely. 'Please explain it. I'm not accustomed to being called devious, so your explanation had better be good.'

CHAPTER EIGHT

THERE was a tense silence as they stared at each other across the table, the grim lines about Lucas's mouth telling Sylvia she had definitely pierced his pride by hinting at this slur on his integrity.

'I'm asking you to explain those words,' he reminded her.

'Very well. The situation has now become clear to me—and I think I can understand your reason for inviting them to join us. You want to see the *other* Maureen.'

He frowned, puzzled. 'Come again?'

'At work Maureen is efficient and impersonal, her mind taken up with the job. But you'd like to see her at play and in a more relaxed mood. Isn't that it?'

'You should go in for detective work.' His voice was sarcastic.

Sylvia ignored his tone. 'It means you really are interested in her, in more ways than one.'

'What are you trying to say?'

'I mean in more ways than as a business partner, of course.' She drew a sharp breath as this thought became firmly planted in her mind. 'Amy will be delighted.'

Lucas leaned forward as he gritted, 'Amy has been told to mind her own business, as I've mentioned before.'

'I'm not sure that Amy and Maureen will be one hundred per cent compatible—I mean, living in the same house—but no doubt Amy will find a flat for herself nearer town.'

'What are you going on about?' he snarled, the glitter in the dark eyes indicating his suppressed anger.

She went on affably, 'When you're married, of course. Naturally you'll want to have the house to yourselves.'

'You're suggesting I'd fling Amy out on her ear?'

'Of course not. I'm merely suggesting that Amy might prefer to find somewhere else to live.'

'Why should she do that? The house has been her home for years.'

'I doubt if you realise the extent of Maureen's dominance. She's accustomed to bossing people, whereas Amy is sweet and gentle, although I suspect that deep down she has a stubborn streak that won't stand for being bossed.'

'At least you're right about the stubborn streak,' Lucas admitted on a grim note, then he looked at her thoughtfully. 'So what suggestion can you make?'

Sylvia shook her head. 'I wouldn't presume to offer any advice. It's for you—and Maureen—to decide.'

He leaned forward, looking at her intently. 'Let me re-phrase the question. What would you do if you suddenly found yourself to be mistress of that house? I mean as far as Amy is concerned.'

'I'd be on my knees begging her to stay.'

'Why?'

'Because I like Amy and would want her to be with—us. Nor could I bear to see her leave the place that had been her home for so long.'

'Yes? Anything else?'

'Oh, there'd be other reasons,' she replied evasively and without looking at him.

'Such as——?' he persisted.

She hesitated to voice the further thoughts in her mind, then decided to be frank. 'Well, I dare say there'd be children. It would be a pity to deny Amy the joy of holding babies, and of being able to help rear your children.'

'You think she'd like to do that?'

'Of course—she'd adore it. But no doubt Maureen will be more than capable of coping with these matters.'

'You're right. Maureen is capable of coping with almost anything.'

The thought of it all gave her a pain, and later, when they left the restaurant to drive down the hill, the ache was still with her. Nor could she find the heart to make cheerful conversation, her silence remaining unbroken until Lucas turned off the main road before entering the city.

The change of direction caused her to ask, 'Where are we going?'

'Home.' The reply came laconically.

'Home? You mean to your house?'

'That's right. Didn't Amy ask for extra nighties? I thought you could choose a couple that are suitable for this time of the year. She might need them, even if she's going home on Sunday.'

When they reached the house he left the car at the kerbside, then led her along the path where the polyanthus sent its perfume into the night air. His key opened the front door, then a switch illuminated the hall from a central chandelier, its light enabling Sylvia to gaze at paintings she had been unable to examine during her first hasty visit to the house.

Lucas noticed her interest. 'Grandfather was a collector,' he explained. 'He loved the pastels and watercolours painted by some of the early New Zealand artists. We have more in the lounge and dining-room. Would you like to see them?'

He led her to where other paintings hung on the walls, and as she admired the works reflecting the country's early settlement she also noticed the valuable ornaments, the quality furniture, and the wall-to-wall carpet that extended through every room.

He led her upstairs to where the four bedrooms overlooked views of the lake and the city lights dancing in the water. In Amy's room the nightdresses were easy to find, and Sylvia slipped them into a plastic carrier bag which happened to be lying on a chair.

Lucas said, 'You may as well see the rest of the house. Would the master bedroom interest you?' Without waiting for her to reply he guided her into what was obviously his own room. 'Not in a very orderly state, I'm afraid,' he grinned, 'but at least it looks lived in, which is more than can be said for those rooms downstairs.'

She looked at the bookshelf and at the phone beside the bed, then said, 'The rooms downstairs look as if they're seldom used. They have a lonely atmosphere in them, but here you have companionship.'

His brows shot up. 'Companionship? Are you saying I bring female company here? Are you suggesting I've used the nighties as a reason for enticing you here?'

She coloured slightly. 'No, of course not. I mean that here you have books and—and the phone.' *Had* he used the nighties as an excuse? she wondered.

He went on drily, 'I haven't noticed much actual warmth issuing from books or from the phone.'

'Books can be good companions,' she pointed out, knowing quite well that this was not the type of companionship he needed. Then she added nervously, 'Isn't it time you were taking me home?'

He ignored the question by asking another. 'Did you enjoy this evening—despite a few negative moments?'

'Oh, yes, very much. Thank you for taking me out.'

'Would a small reward be too much to expect?'

'A re-reward?' Sylvia glanced at the bed and knew sudden panic. 'Wh-what sort of a reward?'

'Just a tiny kiss, as a mark of appreciation.'

She recalled the last time he had kissed her. Her own response had almost sent her up in flames, but she told herself that this time she would keep a firm grip on her emotions. 'Just—just a tiny one,' she said faintly, then raised her face.

His lips were warm on her own, brushing them gently from side to side in a seductive manner that made her want to cry out for more. And then a convulsive movement of his arms snatched her closer to him and the kiss deepened.

Her pulses leapt as he parted her lips. Her arms moved of their own accord to entwine about him. Her eyes closed as his hand on her breast sent sensations shooting through her body. Every nerve became as taut as a violin string, while the plastic bag containing Amy's nightdresses dropped to the floor unnoticed.

Vaguely, Sylvia tried to tell herself to protest, to draw back and run down the stairs, but somehow she lacked the power to do so and, stirring gently, she could only murmur, 'That's a tiny kiss?'

'So far, very tiny,' Lucas responded, then moulded her body against his own.

After that she gave herself up to the bliss of being wafted towards heaven while knowing that his heart thumped against her own. And then a gasp escaped her as her feet literally left the floor. His arms swung her up and, cradling her as he would a child, he carried her to the bed, where he laid her gently on the cover. In an instant his length was stretched beside her, and before she could protest his lips had again covered her own.

And now she knew she was in real danger, not only from the desire that fired his male needs, but also from her own passion that had developed into a deep yearning that positively screamed for fulfilment.

Sylvia had never known what it was like to want a man to this extent, and now the knowledge tore at her, while her willingness to throw caution to the winds registered in her mind sufficiently to frighten her. Yet despite her fears small moans of pleasure escaped her as his lips trailed from her throat to kiss her breast, bared by pushing aside the violet material of her dress.

Nor could she find the power to draw back from the arousal that pressed against her body. The call to her own needs was overwhelming, making it impossible to find the strength to push away the hands that gripped her buttocks.

But suddenly it ended. The bedside phone rang, bringing them both down to earth with a crash. The sound cutting the air with shrill persistence brought an oath from Lucas as he turned on his back.

'Let it ring,' he muttered.

'It could be important,' she whispered, then wondered why it was necessary to whisper. The person at the other end of the line could not know she was on the bed with Lucas.

He thought for a moment, then lifted the receiver. 'Hello?' There was a pause before he exclaimed, '*Maureen*—why the hell are you ringing me? There was another pause while he listened, then exasperation escaped him as he gritted, 'Of course I hadn't forgotten. OK, thank you. *Goodnight.*' The receiver was slammed down.

'That was Maureen?' Sylvia asked unnecessarily.

'Yes. She wanted to remind me that I have an appointment tomorrow morning with a man who'll be in Rotorua for the weekend. As if I'd forget!' snorted Lucas, irritated.

'That wasn't her reason for ringing,' Sylvia said quietly.

'No?' He turned to stare at her. 'Then why did she phone?'

'To learn if you were here. She knows Amy's at my mother's place, and she was curious to know whether you'd taken me straight home or had brought me here. She's probably guessed you have a phone next to the bed and that you were right beside it, with me on the bed. Well, I'm not any longer.' She sprang to the floor, then added, 'Please take me home.'

'OK, OK, I can see the cord has been snapped,' he said ruefully.

'You mean the cord that would bind us together for a few moments only—at least until you remembered that the past is past and not to be started again.'

He stared at her wordlessly.

She went on, 'You see, I haven't forgotten your warning, and I should be grateful to Maureen. Her phone call brought me to my senses.'

'You needed bringing to your senses?' he asked, his voice low.

Sylvia nodded, unable to deny it, yet afraid to look at him.

'Good.' The word held satisfaction. 'It's time you let yourself go emotionally.'

'With you, I suppose?'

'Of course.'

'So that you may have your revenge?'

'*Revenge?*' he echoed. 'Please give me credit for having matured sufficiently to realise you weren't ready for marriage seven years ago.'

'At least that's something to be thankful for, although I must say I find you hard to understand.'

'In what way?'

'Well, your—your actions say one thing, yet your words say something different. I'm probably being quite stupid in trying to follow the trend of your mind.'

'The trend of my mind interests you?' The dark eyes watched her intently.

'When it takes the wrong track concerning my intentions towards yourself it—it makes me feel resentful,' Sylvia explained. 'It causes me to become stiff and unnatural with you, and I have to guard my tongue lest you imagine I'm angling towards a more familiar footing.'

'That same tongue seems to be loose enough now,' he drawled.

'That's probably due to the combination of sherry and wine at dinner,' she excused. 'I'm not really accustomed to drinking much.'

'Your response on the bed was also due to the wine? Remind me to get in a couple of crates!'

Sylvia ignored his banter by going to the window, where she stood staring at the city lights across the water.

Lucas moved to stand beside her, his head bending towards her ear, his voice still low as he murmured, 'That delicious arching towards me was merely the result of too much imbibing?'

The words caused her to catch her breath. She *had* arched towards him because it had been beyond her power to conceal her crying need to be even closer to him.

'Well? You haven't answered the question.'

Vainly she sought for a reply, one that would satisfy not only Lucas but also herself. But despite her ponderings the same admission leapt into her mind. She yearned to reach out to him. It was as simple as that.

But how to answer the question? To admit the truth would confirm his suspicions. It would tell him she desired to turn back the clock, and that this had been her objective in accepting the job in his office. In short, she'd come to heel. And this was something Lucas would soon realise unless she could leave the intimacy of this room, so she turned to him, her eyes wide with appeal as she repeated her former plea. 'Lucas, please take me home.'

His hands gripped her shoulders while he stared down into her upturned face. 'It's not late. You're sure you really want to leave this place just yet?'

Sylvia nodded, knowing that to indicate otherwise would be fatal. He'd have her back on the bed in an instant. But although she tried to free herself of his hands their grip tightened.

'Not so fast,' he muttered, his voice husky. 'First I need one more kiss.' And instead of releasing her his hands drew her closer, then slid down her body, caressing the violet material which in some strange way wrapped itself about his legs almost as though binding them together.

Nor did he kiss her at once, but took his time by gazing down into her face before his lips brushed gently across her closed lids. His mouth moved to nibble the lobe of one ear, then fastened on her own lips with a sensual teasing that forced them apart.

The pressure of his hands in the small of her back made her aware of his inflamed desire, causing an answering fire of response to sear her senses. She felt limp, her knees almost buckling beneath her, but just as she expected to be swept up and laid on the bed again a shuddering breath escaped him.

His hands returned to her shoulders with a firm grip, then dropped to his sides as he stepped back from her. 'So you want to go home. Then let's go.' Bending swiftly, he snatched up the plastic bag containing Amy's nightdresses, then stood back to allow her to precede him through the door.

Still in a daze, Sylvia felt shaky as they went down the stairs, making it necessary to grip the banister.

Lucas noticed the action and took her arm. 'You're all right? You appear to be a little unsteady.'

She felt grateful for his support. 'It's just that I'm not used to—to——' Her words faltered.

'To being brought to the verge of making love?' The words came softly as his hand beneath her chin turned her face towards him.

She returned his stare. 'Did you imagine it to be a nightly occurrence?' She immediately regretted the question.

The drive home was taken almost in silence, and when he accompanied her up the steps to the front door his face remained unsmiling as he said, 'See you tomorrow.'

She nodded dumbly, then stood watching as he backed the car towards the road. The headlights illuminated the garden, but moments later all was in darkness.

Sylvia remained still, looking towards the shadows. This is how it will be, she thought sadly. After next Friday when I've left the office there'll be shadows, gloom, darkness. And then a more truthful thought caused her to whisper to herself, 'Don't you mean when you've left Lucas?'

Later, as she lay in bed, she reviewed the evening. Had it been a success or a disaster? she wondered, staring at the darkened ceiling. There had been definite highlights, she admitted, recalling moments that made her go hot all over, but there had also been moments of depression.

Could the new violet dress be blamed for the latter? Perhaps Amy's vague disapproval had stemmed from the low cut of its cleavage-revealing neckline. And had the hint of rounded breasts caused Lucas to imagine she was ready to be tossed on to the bed? Were they the reason he had been ready to oblige—and would have obliged even further if the phone hadn't rung?

It had been easy to guess that Maureen had watched them leave the restaurant, nor had the questions in her mind been hard to follow. Where would Lucas take Sylvia? she would ask herself. Straight home to Sophia Street, or to his own home from which his aunt was conveniently absent? Was it idle curiosity or something deeper that had sent Maureen to the phone?

Query after query tantalised Sylvia's mind, dancing through her brain like bubbles that burst before answers could be found until at last she told herself her values had slipped out of proportion. Yes, that was it. She was giving too much importance to matters that were not really serious. Amy's disapproval, for instance. What did it matter? And the fact that Lucas might have had a motive in taking her to Aorangi Peak. Was it important?

He had shown her through his home, and the tour of the rooms had engendered an intimacy between them, especially when he had pointed out small treasures that had belonged to his parents. He had lifted her on to his bed where they had almost made love, but still there had been no mention of her remaining in the job.

And then she told herself to be reasonable. Surely, during those moments of closeness, work had been the last thing on his mind, although the phone call from Maureen should have sent his thoughts back towards the office.

She sighed deeply, realising that her previous conviction had been correct. He simply didn't want her to be there, and the knowledge caused her to squirm with frustration and bitter disappointment.

See you tomorrow, he'd said without even bothering to kiss her again when they had reached the door. Well, tomorrow would be another day when she would have the opportunity to be near him. Perhaps it would be a happier day—if only she could take care to guard her sometimes stupid and unruly tongue.

Next morning Sylvia woke with a feeling of expectancy, and for a few minutes lay wondering what the day held in store. The curtain moved gently in the soft breeze that sent high white clouds across the blue, and then the expectancy switched to a subdued excitement. Mokoia Island—with Lucas! Even the recollection that they would not be alone failed to dampen her spirits.

She sprang out of bed, showered and washed her hair, then tried to decide between wearing her red leisure suit or a pale blue one. Her ice-maiden suit, she called the latter because, with her blonde hair, it endowed her with a look of cool cleanliness.

She set about the usual tasks attended to during Wiki's weekend absence, and had almost finished preparing the lunch trays when Lucas arrived.

He followed her into the kitchen where she continued her work with the trays, and although she did her best to appear nonchalant his presence made her feel tense.

He was casually dressed in well-cut trousers and a navy shirt which was sufficiently open at the neck to reveal the short crisp hairs on his chest, and even as she averted her eyes from them she became aware that he was taking an interest in her own attire.

His voice faintly amused, he queried, 'This ice-blue outfit is an indication of today's frigid mood?'

Sylvia turned surprised eyes upon him. 'Are you saying you think I'm a cold person? I thought that—last night—I'd demonstrated otherwise.' The last words had brought a flush to her cheeks, then she added hastily, 'I can change into a red suit if you object to this particular colour.'

Lucas regarded her gravely. 'I haven't yet reached the stage of dictating what you wear. Nor do you need a red suit to remind me that deep down you're a warm person.'

'Thank you—that's a relief.'

'I've also learnt that you have hidden heat that only needs to be encouraged to the surface——'

Further comment was curtailed abruptly by the sudden opening of the back door, and as Sylvia turned she exclaimed with surprise. 'Wiki, have you forgotten it's Saturday?'

'No, I have not. I just come for my best apron with the frills. It's in the drawer where your mother says I can keep my things. I got a job on this evening, eh.'

The Maori woman's plump figure was encased in a floral dress splashed with bright reds, yellows and blues. Her round face was the colour of coffee and cream, and while she beamed at Sylvia her brown eyes also flashed an appraising glance over Lucas.

Sylvia performed a hasty introduction. 'Wiki, this is Mr Carville. Lucas, this is Mrs Matenga.'

Lucas went towards the Maori woman, his hand outstretched. 'I'm pleased to meet you. Sylvia has spoken about you.'

Wiki gave a pleased smile. 'She has, eh? You her boss, eh?'

Sylvia cut in, 'What is this job, Wiki?'

'Oh, a special meal for a bunch of tourists. All Maori type food—specially the seafood and the eel—the *puha* you white people call sour thistle, and the *kumara* you say is the sweet potato. Everything cooked Maori fashion.'

'You mean in a big hole in the ground with hot stones?' Sylvia asked.

'That's right, in the *hangi*. I got to be handing round the food, so I must have my best apron.'

Sylvia watched her take the article from a drawer beneath the bench, then said impulsively, 'We're going to Mokoia this afternoon.'

Wiki examined the state of the apron to make sure it was clean, then glanced from Sylvia to Lucas. 'You are, eh? Then you make sure you pay respect to Matua Tonga.'

Lucas was mystified. 'Who the heck is he?'

'He's the *kumara* god on the island,' Wiki explained. 'He was put there in olden days to make sure the *kumara* crop grow well. To those early people the *kumara* was what you white people call the bread of life, so he very important fellow, eh.'

Enlightenment dawned on Lucas. 'I presume you're referring to that hunk of carved sandstone?'

Wiki nodded, her face serious. 'That's him. There is also a wishing rock on Mokoia, but many of our people prefer to tell a wish to Matua Tonga. You'll see him along the track from that warm pool where Hinemoa lie till Tutanekai come to her.'

'I'll look forward to having a chat with the old fellow,' grinned Lucas.

Wiki caught his amusement. 'No need for you to smile. That *kumara* god got more power than people give him credit for. I tell you that, eh.'

'I'll put him to the test,' Lucas promised quietly.

Wiki went on the defensive. ''Course, not *every* wish come true. Only ones that are good for people.'

'You're saying that disappointment can hover overhead? OK, I've been warned. However, the particular wish I have in mind should be good for more than one person——'

'And especially for business,' Sylvia put in, the words slipping out before she could stop them.

The dark brows rose as Lucas turned to her. 'Naturally, one works better when one is happy.'

'And naturally your wish concerns Maureen,' she pointed out, unable to keep the words from tumbling out or the hint of accusation from her voice.

Wiki's alert brown eyes moved from one to the other, then, almost as though sensing Sylvia's inner depression, she sent her a sideways glance as she said, 'Some of our older people always take their problems to Matua Tonga. Even if you a white person he might fix things for you.'

Lucas hid a smile. 'I'd like to know how he goes about these miracles, Mrs Matenga.'

Wiki looked at him seriously. 'You white people don't understand. It's not really him what does the job. He just gives his orders to all those spirits flying about, eh.'

'Spirits?' Lucas remained unsmiling.

Wiki became defensive. ''Course there's spirits. They're everywhere—specially over at Mokoia.' She went towards the door. 'I go now to help get the food ready for tonight. Soon as I've gone you two can laugh your heads off at this Maori woman and her *kumara* god—and her spirits.' A slight bang of the door echoed her indignation.

Sylvia suppressed a giggle as she said, 'Wiki might have her funny ideas, but she's a genuine person and a tower of strength to Mother.'

Lucas said, 'According to Amy she's what's known as a real treasure—which reminds me, it's time I paid my respects in the number one bedroom.'

After lunch they spent a short period with Amy. However, the older woman offered no approval of the trip to Mokoia until Sylvia offered further information.

'Maureen and Brian are coming with us,' she said impulsively. 'We're to meet them at the jetty.'

Amy's face brightened visibly as she turned to Lucas. 'Well now, that'll be nice. I'm glad Maureen will be with you. Now I know you'll have a happy day.'

'You do? Then let me tell you, you're way off beam,' he snarled.

'No, I'm not, dear,' she returned quietly. 'I'm right on the beam. You can believe it or not.'

Later, as they drove along Fenton Street and turned towards the lakeside jetty, Sylvia made a determined effort to push Amy's words from her thoughts. This was what had happened last night, she recalled. Amy's attitude and remarks had got under her skin. They had played their part in spoiling the evening. Well, she would not allow them to ruin this afternoon.

Lucas sent her a side glance. 'Amy didn't upset you too much?' he queried, almost reading her thoughts.

She became wary. 'Upset me? How could she do that?'

'You know what I mean.'

'You mean by being pleased that Maureen will be with us? I think she's merely pushing you towards the course she considers is best for you.'

'*Pushing* being the operative word,' he muttered tersely.

'Towards Maureen,' Sylvia added, then sat frowning while she wondered how Amy, who looked on Lucas as a son, could want to see him in a close relationship with

Maureen. After all, he really didn't need Maureen. He was a successful man without her, and Amy's idea of a partnership was quite unnecessary. So what was her real aim?

The questions were brushed from her mind as they reached the jetty where Brian and Maureen stood laughing happily together. And as Sylvia's eyes took in the colour of Maureen's red leisure suit she was glad to be wearing her ice-blue trousers and top. Peeping at Lucas, she teased, 'At least one of us is in red—and ready to offer warmth.'

To which he made no reply at all.

The *Ngaroto* lay moored beside the jetty. She was a launch built specially for tourists, her facilities enabling drinks and lunches to be served. Shelter from the hot sun or chilly winds was provided by a long, windowed cabin which stretched from midship to stern, while a view of the waters ahead could be had from the bow.

Lucas parked the car, and as they walked along the jetty greetings were exchanged. Brian's eyes went to Sylvia, while Maureen turned a glowing face towards Lucas. They went aboard accompanied by a party of tourists, and within a short time a muted throb came from below as the vessel edged from the jetty. Smoothly it made its way across the calm waters that lay like a blue jewel in a setting of surrounding green hills.

As they sailed towards the deeper waters of the lake a recorded voice related the story of Hinemoa and Tutanekai, and, while most of the tourists stood listening in silence, Sylvia heard scarcely a word of it. This was because, from the moment of stepping aboard, she had been gripped by an overwhelming wave of nostalgia which took her back over the years.

She knew that Brian and Maureen stood near the bow, his hand on her shoulder while he indicated various points of interest on shore, and she also knew that Lucas stood listening politely. But the sadness that now washed over her caused her to move astern where she stood gazing unseeingly towards the jetty they had recently left.

The last time she had stepped from it to board the *Ngaroto* her parents had been with her. It had been Mother's birthday, she recalled, and in the morning Daddy had announced that he was taking them out for the day.

'Where are we going?' Ruth and Sylvia had asked.

'You'll discover that when we get there,' he had told them. 'It's to be a mystery trip. Only the organiser knows the destination.'

He had driven them for about eleven miles along the eastern shore of Lake Rotorua, stopping at Tikitere, otherwise known as Hell's Gate because of its frenzy of underground activity. Entering the reserve, they had made their way along paths winding between boiling mud pools that broke the greyish-white silica-encrusted ground.

Sylvia recalled that her father had taken her mother's hand while leading her along tracks between sulphurous vents surrounded by brilliant yellow, and the seething cauldrons of this most violent of all the thermal areas. And near the end of the square mile reserve they had made their way to the hot waterfall which tumbled into a pool said to be full of curative powers for all aches and pains.

After he had walked them round Hell's Gate she recalled her father driving them back to Rotorua, where he had taken them to lunch at an expensive restaurant, and by early afternoon he had had them at the jetty in readiness for a trip to Mokoia. At that time he had appeared to be so well, and now as she thought of the hidden danger that had been surrounding his heart, tears filled her eyes and trickled down her cheeks.

She dabbed at them hastily, suddenly aware that Lucas had come to stand beside her. His presence caused her to take a grip on her control, and, pushing the past from her, she blew her nose and waited for him to comment on the tears he had observed.

His deep voice came softly, 'Don't let him upset you to that extent. He's doing it on purpose.'

His meaning escaped her, causing her to turn and stare at him blankly. 'What are you trying to say?'

'I see traces of tears. I presume they're because of Brian, and his attentions to Maureen.'

'How can you be so stupid?' she snapped, irritated.

'Then explain them,' he demanded.

'If you must know, I was thinking about my father.'

'I see.' His tone had become cynical.

'The last time I was on the *Ngaroto* was when he took Mother and me on a mystery trip.' Her eyes filled again.

He made no reply. Instead he turned to observe Brian and Maureen, who were still in the bow.

Sylvia flashed a glare of anger at him. 'It's all right, you don't have to tell me you think I'm lying. It's written all over you. I *know* you don't believe I was just—remembering.'

'To be honest, I suspect you're a trifle upset over our friends. It probably irks you to see them standing so close together,' said Lucas.

She followed his gaze to where the couple stood among other tourists, the tall fair-haired man looking down into Maureen's face while she smiled up at him.

A sudden laugh escaped Sylvia as she said with insight, 'They're trying to make us jealous. It's possible Brian is working on me, while Maureen is definitely working on you. Have you mentioned this partnership idea to her?'

'Certainly not.' The words came harshly.

'Oh, well, I suppose there's plenty of time.'

'Time for what? Please explain yourself,' he snapped.

'Time for you to realise just how much she means to you, of course. Tell me, how is it that a man who's so astute concerning his business affairs can be so dim regarding his own emotional affairs?'

Lucas's jaw tightened. 'I take it you're referring to me?'

'Of course. Who else?' Sylvia smiled to soften the suggestion.

'Are you hinting that I'm emotionally dead?'

'No, just emotionally blind to—to whatever is perhaps best for you. Amy seems to think it's Maureen.'

'But you don't?' He regarded her intently.

'I—I really don't know,' she admitted, finding herself out of her depth and not knowing what to say.

CHAPTER NINE

LUCAS remained at her side while the launch cut through the still waters of the lake. He appeared to have lapsed into a thoughtful frame of mind, his silence making Sylvia wonder if her remarks were causing him to take a closer look at his feelings towards Maureen. But if this was so, his ponderings were interrupted by the *Ngaroto* edging its stern towards the small jetty at Mokoia.

The tourists, who consisted mainly of parents and children, were shepherded along a path towards Hinemoa's pool. They were followed by Brian and Maureen, while Sylvia and Lucas walked at a leisurely pace in the rear.

Looking about her, Sylvia thought that nothing had changed since her last visit. The warm, almost rectangular pool was fringed by flat slabs of rock, and sheltered by pohutukawa trees that would be a mass of crimson bottlebrush-type flowers at Christmas time. At the end of their blooming they would fall, to cover the ground and the pool with a fine red dust.

A few moments were spent in watching children splash in the pool, then Maureen said, 'There's a wishing rock along one of these tracks. I intend to make a wish.'

'But don't expect it to come true,' warned Sylvia. 'That rock is a fraud. I've no faith in it.'

'Sometimes we don't deserve our wishes,' Lucas pointed out. 'We've done nothing to earn them.' He turned to Sylvia. 'Do you remember your last wish, even if it didn't come true?'

'I certainly do.' She turned away, recalling how she had wished for her father to reach a ripe old age, despite his heart condition. But he had not done so. However, she had no desire to go into details, so she said, 'Wiki says the *kumara* god has more power than the wishing rock.'

Maureen laughed. '*Kumara* god? What utter rot! And who, may I ask, is Wiki?'

'She comes during the week to help Mother,' Sylvia explained.

'Are you saying you listen to the superstitions of a Maori servant?' sneered Maureen in a tone filled with derision.

'We don't look on Wiki as a servant,' Sylvia told her quietly. 'Mother finds her quite indispensable.'

'Nobody is indispensable,' Maureen declared loftily. 'Not even you. When you leave the office you'll be replaced immediately. Isn't that so—boss?' She sent a laughing glance towards Lucas.

He did not return her smile. Instead he frowned as he said in a cool voice, 'I doubt that Sylvia will remain unemployed for long.'

Brian spoke to Sylvia, his voice betraying surprise. 'You're leaving? You didn't tell me.'

'No, I didn't see the necessity.'

Brian sent Lucas an enquiring look. 'You've given her the sack, old boy?'

'Of course not. She's leaving because apparently she no longer wishes to be employed by me.'

Brian laughed. 'You must have made a pass at her! She takes a dim view of a boss who gets too fresh.'

A muscle tightened in Lucas's cheek. 'You're overstepping yourself, Brookes,' he snapped.

Brian ignored the reprimand as he stepped closer to Sylvia. Looking down into her face, he said earnestly, 'You do understand that I want you back at the agency? You can return as soon as you've left Carville's hotbed of high technology.'

Lucas snarled, 'This is neither the time nor the place for such discussion. The launch leaves within a certain time, and I intend to walk round the island—with Sylvia.'

His last words sent a glow through her—a glow quickly dampened by the sudden spark of anger that flashed from Maureen's grey eyes. The reason for it was easy enough to guess. She herself had been brought here by Lucas, while Maureen was in the company of Brian. It was a situation that did not suit Maureen, but the irritating circumstances were swept aside as the office senior spoke with forced gaiety.

'I intend to find that wishing rock. I have a very important wish to make. To the devil with the *kumara* god.' She left them, almost running along the path, but was quickly followed by Brian, whose long strides enabled him to catch her within moments.

Sylvia and Lucas followed at a slower pace, their feet making only a soft rustle on the leaf-strewn path. Tall trees rose on either side, towering above a thick undergrowth of native shrubbery and ferns, while the silence was broken by birdsong and the faint voices of tourists who had remained beside the pool.

Little was said, and, peeping at Lucas, Sylvia wondered about his thoughts after that exchange with Brian. Now was his opportunity to ask her to stay—*now was his opportunity*. The words hammered in her head as she did her utmost to send a telepathic message of her yearning to stay in the job.

But he didn't hear it. He merely stood still, gazing upward as he said, 'Have you ever seen such lofty tree-ferns?'

She stared up at the green umbrella fronds arching from the tops of trunks hung with dried brown branches that had not yet fallen. Her eyes blurred and she knew she must accept the situation caused by her own pride.

After walking a distance they came to an opening where seagulls circled overhead, and where Sylvia paused to stare upward. 'There they are!' she exclaimed. 'Wiki's spirits.' Then, looking towards the side path, 'And there *he* is—Matua Tonga.'

'At least we must acknowledge the old fellow,' said Lucas with mock-seriousness.

They went towards the lump of sandstone that had been carved to represent a small, squat human figure, and, although it needed little imagination to see the resemblance, Sylvia found herself wondering why the Maori people felt so sure it had powers of any description. Nevertheless there was something about the small grotesque form that gripped her own imagination.

Lucas said, 'Look at the grin on his face. He knows you're about to make a wish.'

'Or is he leering at my stupidity?'

'Be careful, you might hurt his feelings.'

'You'll make a wish too? You said you had one in mind.'

'I might just let him prove his ability—although I usually rely on my own efforts. Perhaps we should make our wishes together.'

Unexpectedly he moved to stand close beside her. His hand found her own, the firm clasp of his fingers sending a feeling of warmth through her body. She longed to look up into his face, yet feared her own expression might reveal too much, so she closed her eyes, and, taking a deep breath, forced a single line of desperate thought to race through her mind.

Oh, Matua Tonga, she pleaded silently, if you have any powers at all, please make Lucas ask me to stay in the job. Make him ask me to change my mind about leaving—*please*, make him want me to stay!

She opened her eyes and stared at the grinning sandstone face. Why do you want this wish? it seemed to ask.

She closed her eyes again, her mind answering the silent query. It's because I want to be close to him. I want to share his lucky breaks as well as his disappointments. I want to be part of his life. It's because I love him—yes, yes, *I love him*. Please, *please*, Matua Tonga, make him love me!

At last she opened her eyes as the significance of her wishful thoughts hit her with full force.

And then Lucas's voice murmured in her ear, 'That wish seemed to take a long time. It must be important.'

She turned to find him regarding her intently. 'Yes, it was like something becoming clear in my mind.' Then, feeling shaken, she turned away, afraid to look at him while making the effort to cope with her own emotional shock.

Ever since they had stood beneath the cedar tree Sylvia had suspected she might be falling in love with Lucas, but not until these moments had she admitted the truth of the matter—not even to herself. And now that she faced it openly in her mind she didn't know what to do. After all, what *could* she do? Nothing—absolutely nothing.

Lucas regarded her critically. 'Are you all right? You're looking rather pale—almost as if you've just had a shock. Don't tell me the old fellow spoke to you.'

Sylvia laughed shakily. 'Of course he didn't—and of course I'm all right. But I think we should return to Hinemoa's pool. It's the place where they count heads before leaving the island.'

As they continued along the track she noticed he had dropped her hand, and while she longed to reach out and clasp his fingers she resisted the temptation. However, different thoughts were forced to enter her mind when they reached the pool where Maureen and Brian sat waiting.

Maureen frowned as they approached. 'Where have you been?' she demanded with barely concealed irritation. 'I thought you'd have caught up with us ages ago.'

'We paused to talk to the *kumara* god,' Lucas explained lightly.

'Him!' Maureen scoffed crossly. 'I've more faith in the wishing rock. It would have been fun if we could have all wished there—I mean *together*.' She sent a meaningful glance towards Lucas.

Sylvia looked at her curiously, sensing that beneath the surface Maureen was seething with suppressed anger. Had she become bored with Brian? Had he annoyed her in some way? She turned to where a few children still splashed in the pool while their parents stood chatting in groups, then, moving a short distance away, she gazed sightlessly across the lake. Again she felt shaken by the awareness of her love for Lucas, the impact being sufficient to send a tremor through her.

Brian's voice spoke beside her. 'Something's bothering you, Sylvia?' He had moved to her side unnoticed.

Startled, she said, 'No—why should there be anything wrong?'

'That's all right, then. Carville and I don't want two bitchy women on our hands.'

Her eyes widened with indignation. 'Bitchy? What are you talking about?'

Irritated, he said, 'Maureen has developed a fit of peevishness. I suspect Carville has something to do with it.'

'Oh?' Sylvia became interested.

He gave an exclamation of impatience. 'There was I, doing my best to entertain her with stories of the bloodshed and battles that had been fought on this island, when it dawned upon me she wasn't even listening. She kept looking back to discover why you were taking so long to catch up with us.'

'Is that so?'

'It sure is. Actually, I'm beginning to suspect she's more than casually interested in Carville. What's the emotional situation on his part, do you know?'

'No, I've no idea.' The words came faintly.

'When we reached the hunk of wishing rock she seemed to go off into a trance, closing her eyes and clasping her hands as though talking to St Peter himself.'

'Really?' Sylvia looked at him expectantly. If she kept her mouth shut she might hear more, she decided.

Brian continued to air his grievance. 'When I asked if she'd gone to sleep she snapped at me. Told me to shut up. I couldn't help wondering if her wish was being concentrated on Carville.'

'That should please his aunt,' Sylvia retorted unguardedly.

Brian sent her a look of surprise. 'Mrs Grayson? Where does she come into the picture?'

Brian's words had added fuel to the state of confusion in Sylvia's mind, and without pausing to consider the indiscreet nature of her own words she admitted, 'His aunt would like to see them go into partnership.'

Again he expressed surprise. 'He doesn't impress me as being one who would take in a partner.'

'He doesn't?' Sylvia's spirits rose. 'How can you feel so sure about that? I mean, you don't really know him.'

'I know he's an independent do-it-himself type of man. He prefers to rely on himself, rather than on anyone else. However, it would be nice for Maureen. I must ask her if he's already hinted at the prospect.'

Sylvia was appalled by the thought, then became filled with sudden panic as she pleaded, 'No, please don't say a word to her. It's—it's confidential——'

He laughed. 'It can't be such a great secret if you've been told about it!'

'You don't understand. It's just an idea that's come to his aunt, and he—he hasn't decided yet.'

'But you've heard it discussed?'

'Only very vaguely. I'm sure Maureen doesn't know about it—at least not yet.'

'Then she should be told it's in the wind,' he grinned.

'Only when Lucas comes to a decision about the matter. He's the one who must tell her.'

'She should be given the opportunity to think about it.'

'Naturally she'll be able to do so.'

'I might whisper a word in her ear,' Brian remarked thoughtfully. 'I'll tell her you told me.'

Sylvia became agitated. 'Don't you dare! Lucas would be furious with me.'

Brian sent her another grin. 'You don't say? That would amuse me mightily. I'd like to give that arrogant fellow a poke in the eye. Huh! Him and his *castle*——'

'You're jealous because he's so successful,' Sylvia accused, then became aware of more inner panic as she thought of the result of her careless prattling. 'Lucas would be in a real rage with me for discussing his affairs,' she admitted miserably.

'So, what would that matter, considering you'll no longer be working for him?'

'It matters a great deal to me,' she snapped.

Brian's mouth twisted. 'You're forgetting that *I'm* the one who should matter to you.'

'Is that so? And what about all those others who also matter to you—Maureen among them?'

'You know perfectly well that you're the main one, Sylvie.'

'Am I indeed? How very flattering! Then let me warn that if you so much as breathe one word of this partnership business to Maureen I'll never speak to you again. And as for returning to the estate agency, you can forget it.'

'I can see where your real worry lies,' Brian almost snarled. 'You're afraid of Carville's disapproval. You can't bear to think of his adverse criticism falling on your head.'

Sylvia could find no answer, acknowledging the truth of his words to herself. Lucas would soon learn that she had leaked the information. He would look on her with scorn, knowing she couldn't keep her mouth shut. He'd consider her to be a gossiping idiot who was unable to keep her boss's private or business affairs to herself.

And for him to know that the suggestion of a partnership had reached Maureen through Brian would make matters even worse. It would confirm the fact that she had spread the news because, apart from Amy and himself, she was the only person who knew about it. At least, as far as she knew.

Turning towards the pool, she saw Lucas and Maureen coming slowly towards them. Apprehension gripped her, causing her to whisper urgently, 'Promise you won't say a word about the partnership!'

'Ah, so you plead.' His mouth twisted into a mocking grin that was full of satisfaction. 'Sorry, I can promise nothing. You can call it retaliation.'

Sylvia looked at him wonderingly. 'What are you talking about?'

'Or retribution, if you like, for the previous brush-off attitude you've handed me for so long—especially when you know we should have been married ages ago.'

She gave a derisive laugh as she scoffed, 'A fine husband you would have made!'

Brian's face darkened. 'Just be careful, or I'll blurt it out here and now!'

The warning silenced her. She knew that Brian had a vindictive streak and that revenge would be sweet. He was more than capable of bringing up the subject, and then the day would be ruined for everyone—except Maureen, of course.

But what would be the reaction from Lucas? Would he throw cold water on the pleasant surprise she would receive? Or would he accept the situation and admit he had been thinking about it? Maureen would know that where there was smoke there was fire, and that he must have had it in mind. And unless Brian pointed out this fact, she could not possibly realise the suggestion had come from Amy Grayson, rather than from Lucas.

As the other people reached their side Lucas said, 'It's time to go back to the jetty. Everyone is being rounded up for departure, unless you'd prefer to spend the night on the island,' he added softly in Sylvia's ear.

'Alone?' she asked lightly, knowing he did not speak seriously.

'The nights can be chilly,' he went on in a low voice. 'You couldn't expect old Matua Tonga to keep you warm. That would be my job.'

The thought made her senses swim, but her voice remained steady. 'How would you expect to do that?'

'Just by holding you close to me.'

Her eyes misted unexpectedly as she became consumed by guilt. He was being so nice to her, whereas she herself had let him down by discussing his affairs with Brian Brookes, of all people, for whom Lucas held little regard.

She shuddered to think of his reaction when he learnt of her indiscretion. He would look upon her with disgust. He'd be thankful to see her leave his offices. And then instinct warned that all this would occur within a short time because, despite any promises, Brian would be unable to keep it to himself.

As they walked towards the jetty Brian's voice hit her ears as he spoke to Maureen. 'Have you noticed the many seagulls flying over Mokoia? Legend declares them to be the spirits of the numerous warriors slaughtered on the island.'

Maureen snapped angrily, 'For pity's sake, Brian, you talk of nothing but bloodshed and battles! You've fed them to me for most of the afternoon. Can't you find a more pleasant subject? Can't you think of something I'd *like* to hear?'

Brian gave a sudden shout of laughter, then sent Sylvia a look that made her hold her breath. Grinning, he said,

'Something that would please you? Well, yes, I reckon I could, Maureen old dear.'

Sylvia heard him continue to chortle as though at some secret joke. Her heart skipped a beat because she knew what he meant—and she felt sick.

Little was said during the launch trip back to the mainland. Sylvia stood in the bow watching the city and its surrounding hills draw closer, and as they approached the jetty she looked down to watch the smooth waters being divided into two arms of frothy white foam that swept out from the sides of the lower bow.

Lucas came to stand beside her. 'There's something to intrigue you down there?'

'Only the water. It reminds me of people. They meet for a short time, them something causes them to part. After that they go their own way, never to meet again.'

He regarded her narrowly. 'I'd like to know the cause of this morbid mood. Is it something that Brookes has said?'

She shook her head, longing to say, 'No, it's something *I've* said. Yet despite the opportunity that offered itself she was unable to utter the words.

At the back of her mind lurked a vague hope that she could be worrying needlessly. After all, she couldn't be sure that Brian would tell Maureen of the suggested partnership. And then another thought struck her as she realised the suggestion had initially come from Amy—so wasn't *she* the one to whom an apology was due?

However, this didn't alter the fact that Lucas would be furious with her for blabbing of the affair. She knew it instinctively. And now, watching him from the corner of her eye, she gathered her courage in both hands. She'd confess and get it over.

But it was too late. They had reached the jetty and people were surging forward in readiness to disembark, making it obvious that now was not the moment. Then, as they walked towards the car park, Maureen drew Lucas aside for a few private words.

Watching them, Sylvia felt a rising apprehension which made her turn to Brian. A sharp breath escaped her as she accused, 'You've told her already?'

'As yet I haven't breathed a word,' he assured her.

'Then please don't,' she implored again. 'Promise me.'

The expression on her face caused him to chuckle. 'My goodness, we *are* anxious! We're almost breaking out into a sweat, aren't we?'

The truth of his words kept her silent.

He went on, 'You're failing to see my side of the situation.'

'*Your* side? I can't see that it concerns you.'

'But it does. Surely you can see that if Maureen realises there's been even a whisper of a partnership she might be able to move on her own accord to make it a reality.'

'Oh, yes, I can see that very clearly,' said Sylvia in a tone low enough to conceal its bitterness.

'After settling into a business partnership they could merge into one that's even closer—and *that* would get the thought of him out of your own pretty blonde head. It would give it the chance to turn in my own direction.'

She compressed her lips before a hot reply could be snapped at him. Watch your tongue, stupid, she warned herself, or Maureen will be told almost at once.

Nor did his next words offer any comfort. 'You begin your last week with Carville on Monday, I believe.'

'Yes.' The mere thought made her feel despondent.

'The following week I shall expect to see you back in the agency office—or else.' His tone had become hard.

'*Or else?* Is this a form of blackmail?'

'You may give it any name you like.'

She swung round and left him abruptly, almost bumping into Maureen, who was about to rejoin Brian. And as she walked across the parking area to where Lucas stood waiting beside the Alfa Romeo she knew that her face was still flushed with anger.

His dark eyes held curiosity. 'Something has upset you?'

Sylvia bit her lower lip, then prevaricated, 'It's just Brian, demanding my return to the estate agency on Monday week.'

'What gives him the right to demand?'

'His imagination, coupled with the fact that Brian is a—demander.'

'So you'll spring to attention. You'll jump to his request like an obedient child.' Lucas's voice held derision.

'I—I suppose so.' Her lip trembled slightly.

'Why do I get the feeling there's more to this situation than meets the eye? You know perfectly well you have the ability to obtain a job elsewhere.'

She groped for a reason, then prevaricated, 'Don't forget there's the matter of Mother's affairs.'

'You're using that as an excuse. If it's necessary for her affairs to be examined, the job is for more expert hands than your own,' Lucas pointed out drily.

He was right, and she knew it.

'I can only presume you *desire* to go back there to work beside Brookes. Isn't that so? Why not be honest?'

'No, no, you're quite wrong!' The words escaped like a cry.

'Then what *do* you want?' The question came harshly.

'Just for things to stay as they are,' she confessed in little more than a whisper, then held her breath as she awaited his reply.

But he gave no indication of having heard what she had said. Instead, staring at the road ahead, he remarked, 'I understand that Brookes has plans to make you feel thoroughly at home.'

Sylvia sent him a rapid glance. 'He told you that?'

'No. Maureen told me.'

'Oh.' She felt nettled. 'So she was discussing me with you?'

'Only to point out the inevitable.'

'What would that be?'

'The result of your—er—homecoming to the agency, I suppose. Apparently he'll be making alterations. The girl working there now will be moved into a smaller side room, while you'll take your place in the larger office beside him.'

Anger began to agitate within her, but she remained calm on the surface. 'Got it all nicely settled in his mind, has he?'

'Such would appear to be the case. He's even considering giving you your father's desk which he himself has been occupying——'

'While he acquires a nice new one—something opulent, no doubt,' Sylvia cut in, her irritation beginning to get the better of her. 'Tell me, why did Maureen see fit to acquaint you with the details of Brian's plans for me? Did she imagine you'd be even faintly interested in—in what would be happening to me?'

Lucas's broad shoulders lifted in a slight shrug. 'As I said, she was informing me of the inevitable. Your closer association in the office with Brian is sure to lead to a more intimate relationship.'

'Just as your business partnership with Maureen will lead to—to another sort of commitment.'

He frowned. 'Why should you be so sure of that?'

She sent him her sweetest smile. 'As Maureen says, it's the inevitable.'

The thought of Lucas in a closer association with Maureen filled her with an intense desire to scream. And, although her own association with him was nearing its end, the memory of her own indiscretion bore heavily upon her. It was something she felt compelled to get off her mind, so, as they turned into Sophia Street, she laid a hand on his arm and said, 'Lucas, please stop the car. I need to talk to you.'

His swift glance betrayed surprise, but he said nothing as he drove past her home, then continued until he reached a stretch of open country beyond the end of Sophia Street. They were on a bypass leading to the main highway, and, pulling to the side of the road, he switched off the motor, then twisted in his seat to face her.

'Well?' he demanded, regarding her quizzically.

Sylvia stared down at her hands, not knowing how to begin until at last she muttered, 'I'm afraid you'll be mad with me. If you fly into a rage I'll—I'll quite understand.'

'You consider I'm in the habit of flying into a rage?'

'No, not really——'

'Then why do you expect me to do so now? And why are you avoiding my eyes? You look as guilty as the devil himself.'

'I am. I've—talked too much. I told Brian that Amy is hoping you'll take Maureen into partnership. I'm terribly sorry—it just slipped out.' Her last words came with a rush as she became aware of a feeling of intense relief. It was like dropping a burden, and as she turned to observe his reaction she added, 'I can only repeat I'm terribly sorry—although I've already said so.'

Lucas stared at her thoughtfully before asking quietly, 'Are you afraid I'll be unable to deal with the situation?'

'No, it's not that. You've become a person who can deal with anything. It's my own indiscretion that fills me with remorse. I had no right to divulge anything you have in mind—especially anything of such a private nature.'

'You're so sure you know what I have in mind? Amy's idea is not necessarily my idea—or haven't you noticed that small fact?'

Sylvia turned wide eyes upon him. 'Then you're not really mad with me?'

'Not at all. As it happens I've been giving this partnership idea a great deal of thought.'

'Oh? You have?' She looked down at her hands again. Here it comes, she thought. He's about to tell me the announcement will be made any day now.

As if in confirmation he went on, 'The more I think about it, the more it appeals to me.'

'Does that mean you've come to a definite decision?'

'Yes. I've come to realise that things must be shared if they're to be fully appreciated. Don't you agree?'

'I—I suppose so.'

'You don't sound very enthusiastic. Perhaps you don't agree?'

'Oh, yes, I do agree,' she hastened to assure him. 'Nothing is any good unless it's shared, although it depends——' Her words dwindled into silence.

'It depends on the person with whom it's shared,' Lucas finished for her. 'Isn't that what you were about to say?'

'Surely that goes without saying,' she said, staring ahead and becoming thoroughly miserable. Then, feeling unable to bear any more of this conversation, she turned a bleak face towards him, her voice tremulous as she pleaded, 'Please take me home.'

He made no comment as he switched on the engine and turned the car back towards Sophia Street. They made the short journey in silence, and as he turned into the driveway he said, 'At least your confession clears one puzzle from my mind. It was the smirk on Brookes's face. He was positively burning with satisfaction, and I couldn't help wondering why.'

'That was because I'd been pleading with him to keep the—the hint of the partnership to himself.'

'And he promised to do so?'

'Only if I promised to return to work with him.'

'Backed you into a corner, did he? But now you won't have to go back to his office, because your mind can be cleared of that worry. It won't matter if he tells Maureen.'

'Is it necessary to have further discussion concerning Brian?' Sylvia demanded crossly. 'I think we should go in and see Amy. She'll be most anxious to learn if you've had a happy afternoon with *Maureen*.' Despite herself the last words slipped out, betraying her frustration.

Lucas grinned at her. 'How right you are! In any case, I must learn what time she expects to be taken home tomorrow.'

'Mother will miss her. She's enjoyed having her here. And Mr Mackenzie was due to leave this afternoon. The place will seem empty without them.'

'No doubt Brookes will keep his mother here for as long as possible,' he commented drily.

Sylvia refused to be drawn into making a sharp retort, and instead she smiled sweetly as she said, 'Mother will be expecting you to have your evening meal with us. I hope you'll stay.'

'You do? You're sure of that?'

'Of course. At least for Amy's sake.'

'But not because you have any further desire for my company?'

She was dismayed. 'Why do you say that?'

'Because something still niggles at me. Something I'm unable to sort out, apart from having a strong feeling that it concerns that dratted partnership idea of Amy's. What gives me the strong suspicion that it involves you in some way?'

She opened her mouth to speak, but he silenced her.

'Yes, I know you've told me you had no part in putting the idea into her head, and while I'm trying hard to believe you I also believe she got the idea from you in some way.'

'Then your best plan is to ask her,' said Sylvia. 'Why not go in right now and demand to know exactly how I come into the scene?'

'Right. I'll do that—and you'll come with me.' Lucas grabbed her hand and strode towards the house, causing her to almost run to keep up with him.

CHAPTER TEN

AS THEY reached the front hall the phone began to ring, its echo causing Sylvia to pause and remove her hand from Lucas's grip. 'I'd better answer it,' she said. 'It's probably for Mother.'

He sent her a hard look. 'Very well. I'll go to Amy, but I'll expect to see you within a few minutes.'

She watched him walk along the hall, then lifted the receiver. 'Hello, this is——'

Brian's voice cut her short. 'I know the number exactly, Sylvie.'

She remained silent, wondering what he wanted.

He went on, 'This afternoon I meant to ask you when Mrs Grayson is due to go home.'

'Tomorrow morning.' She paused, puzzled. 'Why do you want to know?'

'You can't possibly guess at the simple answer?'

'No. I can't see why her departure should interest you.'

'Don't be obtuse, Sylvie. While *she's* there—and *he's* visiting each evening—how can I make arrangements for us to go out?'

'Nor can I see how Amy's or Lucas's presence here affects that particular prospect—especially as I have no intention of going out with you.'

His voice came smoothly. 'Aren't you forgetting our little bargain?'

She was appalled. '*That* didn't include going out in the evening!'

'Then you'd better think again, my love, or Maureen will be told about you know what.' Brian went on chattily, 'In fact I've been thinking it over, and I consider it would be helpful for Maureen to have a quiet discussion with Mrs Grayson. Then she could learn at first hand what the dear soul really has in mind.'

Sylvia felt a surge of panic. 'No, no, I don't think that would be a good idea.'

'Actually, I thought of bringing her along this evening. I'll visit my mother while she—I mean Maureen——'

'No, you will not!' Sylvia snapped into the receiver. 'Amy would be upset, and she's not yet in a fit state to be worried.' She took a deep breath to control her anger, then added on a note of subdued triumph, 'As it happens, I've already admitted my thoughtless disclosure to Lucas, so *that* should take some of the roar out of your thunder!'

There was silence at the other end while Brian digested this fact, and during it Sylvia became aware of Lucas leaning nonchalantly against the doorway of the number one bedroom. The sight of him caused her to take a grip on her anger, so she forced a smile and said sweetly, 'As far as *he's* concerned, you're now welcome to do as you please. Goodbye.'

The receiver was replaced with more force than necessary, and as she went towards Lucas she was acutely aware of the flush still staining her cheeks.

He regarded her narrowly. 'What was all that about?'

'It was Brian. He—he hinted at bringing Maureen to talk to Amy about—about what she has in mind.'

'If he does I'll deal with the situation.' The words were snapped crisply.

A sign of relief escaped her. 'Thank heavens I told you about my stupidity!'

'You're saying I'm a shoulder to lean on?'

She nodded, then moved to enter the number one bedroom, but saw it was empty. The bed had been made and there was no sign of Amy.

'I've discovered her to be up and about,' Lucas told her. 'She's enjoying the warmth of the living-room fire, enthroned in the best armchair, no less.'

As they went into the room Amy sent Sylvia a beaming smile. 'Ah, there you are, dear. As you can see, I'm up at last—even if I'm still in dressing-gown and slippers. And your mother insists I have this lovely warm shawl around my shoulders. She said she made it herself—all crochet work done with cream natural wool.'

'Probably straight from the sheep's back,' said Lucas, bending to place a light kiss on Amy's forehead. 'How do you feel?' he asked, the gentleness in his voice betraying the fact that he had real affection for his aunt.

'Somewhat shaky after so many days in bed,' Amy admitted. 'My legs won't seem to hold me up.'

'You'll be ready to come home tomorrow?' he queried.

She hesitated. 'Well, Ruth has invited me to stay a little longer, but I *should* go home——'

Ruth spoke quickly. 'Her legs are weak. I'd like to keep her here until they become stronger.'

Sylvia spoke in agreement. 'You're right, Mother. Amy needs a few more days here before having to cope with going up and down the stairs.'

'You're both very kind,' said Amy in a voice that held a slight tremor as she drew the shawl closer about her shoulders.

Sylvia sent a look of enquiry towards Lucas. Did he intend to continue with his plan to question his aunt concerning herself? she wondered. Or had her mother's presence caused the time to be inopportune?

He caught the query in her eyes, and, as if in answer to her thoughts, he frowned, then shook his head slightly. Now is not the moment, his manner seemed to indicate.

She gave a faint smile, nodding in silent agreement.

Then Ruth said, 'Mr Mackenzie's son and daughter-in-law came to fetch him this afternoon. He'll be living with them in Hamilton. They're a bright young couple—I'm sure he'll be happy with them.'

Amy teased, 'I'm amazed he could drag himself away from you!'

Ruth laughed. 'I'll miss him, but only until the next male convalescent arrives.'

Sylvia made an effort to sound casual as she asked, 'When will Mrs Brookes be leaving?'

'Oh, another couple of days will see her moving much more easily,' said Ruth, glancing at her watch. 'It's time for her evening tray. It's on the bench but is waiting for the dish in the microwave oven to be given a few minutes.'

'I'll see to it,' Sylvia said, then left them and went to the kitchen.

She found Brian's mother sitting up in bed and looking much more comfortable than when she had first arrived. 'I can see the pain is disappearing from your ribs,' she said, making an effort to be cheerful.

'And thank goodness for *that*.' Ellen Brookes declared. She swept a glance over Sylvia's pale blue leisure suit, then demanded testily, 'Where's my son? I know you went to Mokoia with him.'

'And with Lucas and Maureen,' Sylvia reminded her. 'We were a party of four. Brian and Maureen left us at the jetty, so I presume he's taken her home—or perhaps he's taken her out to dinner,' she added casually.

Ellen Brookes's eyes turned to pebbles. 'That doesn't seem to concern you at all.'

Sylvia's eyes widened with surprise. 'No. Why should it?'

'Well, *really*, after the way you've led him on—all this playing hard to get—my poor boy doesn't know where he stands!'

Sylvia's voice became cool. 'Mrs Brookes, I can assure you that as far as I'm concerned Brian knows exactly where he stands.'

'Oh? And where is that, may I ask?'

'Just—as a friend. If he hasn't learnt that fact it's about time he did.' And having adjusted the legs of the tray she had set before Ellen Brookes, Sylvia left the room.

When she returned to the living-room she was surprised to find that Amy had moved to seat herself at Ruth's writing desk. 'I need some clothes,' she explained to Sylvia. 'Don't forget that you brought me here in my nightie and dressing-gown. But if I'm to stay here for a few extra days I can't live in a dressing-gown. I must be able to get dressed so that I can walk round the garden.'

'And along the path beside the golf course,' Lucas put in, his eyes on Sylvia..

The remark caused her to take a quick breath. Was he reminding her of the evening he had held her so closely beneath the spreading branches of the deodar cedar? She hesitated to turn in his direction, yet despite herself her eyes were drawn towards him, then became locked in a gaze with his.

'I haven't forgotten,' she found herself saying.

'Good.' The reply came crisply. 'I thought that perhaps you'd wiped the incident from your mind.'

'Incident? So that's all it was to you?'

Before he could answer, Amy cut in with a hint of impatience. 'Lucas dear, I'm trying to tell you where to find my clothes, but I don't believe you're even listening!'

'I dare say I'll find them in your room somewhere.'

'But will you find the *right* ones?' Amy queried anxiously. 'I'll need my grey woollen suit with the red blouse for going home, and I'll definitely need my coat.'

'Stop worrying! I'll find them,' Lucas told her.

She continued reading aloud from her list. 'Vests—petticoats—witches' britches——'

'What the heck are they?' he cut in.

'My warm bloomers, of course. Sylvia would recognise them at once—wouldn't you, dear?' The question came anxiously.

Sylvia chuckled. 'I should hope so!'

Amy looked at her thoughtfully. 'Would you do me a favour? Would you mind going with Lucas to find these clothes for me? I'm afraid I've no faith in his ability to choose the right garments.'

Sylvia sent a nervous glance towards Lucas. Memory of her last visit swept into her mind, causing her to lick dry lips.

'I'd be so grateful if you'd go with him,' Amy pursued. 'Would it interfere with other things you might have in mind?'

'Of course not,' Sylvia hastened to assure her, then became conscious of an excitement stirred by the thought of another visit to the house above the lake. Even if for only a short time, and to find clothes, it would be a memory to treasure.

'She's been there before,' Lucas reminded his aunt with an amused chuckle. 'She found your nighties without any trouble at all.' He turned to Sylvia. 'I'm sure you remember how quickly you found them?'

This time she was unable to meet his gaze. Oh, yes, she had a vivid memory of that particular scene. Not the speed with which she had found the nightgowns, but the speed with which she had found herself on the bed. And then there had been her rapid rise to a state where the intensity of her yearning to make love had almost overcome her willpower. In fact it had only been the phone——

'You *do* remember?' Lucas persisted softly.

'Yes, of course I remember where I found the nighties,' she said in a voice that was surprisingly normal.

Ruth spoke to Amy. 'Tell her where to look for all the things you need,' she advised.

'I'm doing just that,' said Amy. 'I'm making a few notes to help her find things. Stockings—top left drawer of chest. Suspender belts in same drawer. Undies in other drawers of chest. And I'll need my black brogues for walking outside.' She paused in her writing to look at Lucas. 'You'll take Sylvia to find these things quite soon, dear?'

'This evening, if you like,' he grinned.

The words caused Sylvia's heart to skip a beat, but Amy assured him that such haste was unnecessary. 'Tomorrow morning will do nicely, thank you, dear, and then I'll get dressed for the afternoon.'

He turned to Sylvia. 'Would eleven o'clock suit you?'

'Perfectly. I'll have finished my morning chores by then.'

He took the list from Amy's hand, and after a brief study he said, 'It shouldn't take too long to search for this little lot. A few minutes should see the job done.'

Sylvia heard the words with a sense of disappointment. If it wouldn't take long it meant he had no intention of lingering there with her. And this meant that despite his softly spoken reminder, her previous short visit to that house had meant nothing to him.

The rest of the evening passed in an atmosphere of quiet harmony. Amy returned to bed soon after the evening meal, and with her departure Lucas declared he had a few unfinished matters needing attention in his office. So if Ruth and Sylvia would excuse him, he'd put in an hour's work.

A feeling of inner despair gripped Sylvia as she watched him drive away. There had been no suggestion of a moonlight walk along the path beside the golf course, she noticed. So did this mean he'd had enough of her for one day?

And there was also his statement about Amy's clothes taking no longer than a few minutes to find. Did this mean he had no real wish to be alone with her? It sounded suspiciously as if he meant to hustle her in and out of the house in double-quick time.

The thought of Amy's clothes caused her to recall that she had a confession to make to the older woman, and, wishing to clear her mind of it, she made her way to the number one bedroom, where she found Amy sitting up in bed reading a magazine.

The latter's brows rose as she peered across the top of her glasses. 'Lucas has gone so soon?'

'Yes. He said something about unfinished work at the office.'

'That's disappointing. I came to bed early so that you could have a little more time together.'

It was Sylvia's turn to betray surprise. 'You did? But I'm not Maureen——'

'I know that, my dear, only too well,' Amy sighed.

'But I thought you were anxious to—to see an alliance between Lucas and Maureen.'

'Only to a certain extent, and when he's ready.'

Sylvia hesitated, then took the plunge. 'Actually, that's what I've come to talk about. I'm afraid she might have already been told about your wish to see her in partnership with Lucas.'

Amy's eyes widened with a hint of alarm. 'Told? What do you mean? Are you saying that Lucas has broached the subject?'

'No, he hasn't said a word to her. I'm afraid it's my fault. I spoke rather carelessly to Brian Brookes and I rather suspect that he might tell her.'

Amy looked at her in silence.

Sylvia went on. 'I'm sorry, Amy, it just slipped out. But as the partnership was your idea I felt I had to tell you that Maureen is likely to learn about it perhaps sooner than anyone had intended.'

'Does Lucas know about this?'

'Yes, I've admitted my indiscretion to him. He said he'd deal with it if—if necessary,' Sylvia finished weakly.

'Then there's no need for you to worry about it.' Amy lapsed into a thoughtful silence before she added, 'Perhaps I should come to light with a small confession of my own.'

The words surprised Sylvia. 'Confession? From you?'

'If you must know the truth, I had a purpose in suggesting that partnership to Lucas. Years ago I learnt that to push him in one direction usually meant he moved the opposite way. So I thought that if I tried to push him towards Maureen, he'd automatically turn towards you. It was a spur-of-the-moment idea, but I'm afraid it hasn't worked. It's merely made him very angry. You can't imagine how cross he's been with me,' Amy finished ruefully.

Sylvia could scarcely believe her ears. 'You were really trying to push him towards *me*? Dear Amy, don't you realise he's not even remotely interested in me? I mean, not any longer.'

'Don't you think so? I wouldn't be too sure of that.'

Sylvia bit her lip, then spoke in a low voice. 'You probably don't know I'm the one who refused to marry him seven years ago.'

'Actually, I was aware of the fact.'

Sylvia's cheeks felt warmer. 'You were? *He told you?*'

Amy shook her head and asked, 'Would it surprise you to learn that he's kept a photo of you all these years? I saw it quite by accident and when you walked into my bedroom with those birthday carnations I knew you at once. I couldn't fail to recognise those large blue eyes and that halo of blonde hair. It's really lovely hair. You're indeed fortunate to have been blessed with it.'

Amy's words sent Sylvia to bed in a happier frame of mind. She was pleasantly surprised to learn that Lucas had kept a photo of her, and the knowledge gave her a feeling of inner warmth.

When she woke next morning her spirits were still buoyant. Anticipation filled her as she jumped out of bed, then stood beneath the hot shower where she washed her hair with an expensive shampoo. She rubbed it vigorously before using her blow-drier to set it in a style that emphasised its soft waves and shining tendrils.

The deep blue velvety leisure suit she put on made her eyes look like sapphires, and as she went about her morning chores her heart grew even lighter as the hands of the grandfather clock crept towards eleven.

Lucas arrived as its chimes echoed in the hall. His black trousers hugged the slimness of his hips, while the open neck of his black shirt revealed a triangle of short, crisp dark hairs. His eyes took in every detail of her appearance, resting on her hair before moving to hold her azure gaze with a force that was hypnotic. He made no comment, but the quiet smile hovering about his lips betrayed his approval.

'We'll be back in a short time,' he said to Amy as they were about to leave.

She was sitting in a sunny corner of the living-room, again clad in her warm dressing-gown. 'There's no need for haste,' she assured him. 'I'm quite comfortable at the moment, thank you.'

'Nevertheless, we'll be back soon,' he declared firmly.

Sylvia heard his words with a pang of disappointment. They could mean only one thing: he had little or no wish to be alone with her.

Moments later as he opened the car door for her she questioned, 'You're hoping for this to be a rushed job?'

'It shouldn't take too long,' he returned casually. 'You have Amy's list, I presume.'

'Yes, but a few more items have been added to it. It's possible I might not find these extras as rapidly as you appear to expect.'

'What sort of extras?'

'Oh, she'd like me to bring her mauve woollen dress, but she's not sure where the belt is to be found. And she wants the pearl brooch she wears at the neck of it. She's not sure which trinket box it will be in, so I'll just have to search for it.'

'You'll find everything,' he said with confidence. 'I'll just let you loose in her room.'

The words gave her an uneasy feeling, but she said nothing.

When they arrived at the house they entered through the door leading from the garage into the kitchen. They went through to the front hall, where Lucas took a medium-sized suitcase from a cupboard beneath the stairs, then they went up to the upper rooms.

The silence between them made Sylvia feel uncomfortable. Has something annoyed him? she wondered. Or is it just that he doesn't want to be alone in this house with me? The last thought made her feel cold with misery, turning this longed-for period with him into an anticlimax.

Nor did her spirits lift when he put the suitcase on Amy's bed, opened the lid and said in an offhand manner, 'It's an old case with a loose catch, but with luck it'll hold. I'll leave you to search.'

The words dismayed her. 'You're not staying with me?'

'No. I'll go to the office and collect a few letters that are ready for posting—I'd like them to catch the early mail. If they're in the post office this evening they'll be away first thing in the morning.'

'I see.' Sylvia turned away, almost choking with disappointment. So she had been right: Lucas had no intention of staying alone in the house with her. Was it because of the last time when they had almost made love on his bed? Was he avoiding a repeat performance? Somehow she didn't believe she was in any real danger of such an occurrence.

A sigh escaped her as she went to the window and watched him drive away. And as the car disappeared she realised he was playing for safety by avoiding close contact with her. Of course, the past is past and not to be revived, she recalled. Then, sighing again, she turned to the task in hand.

Most of the items of clothing were easy to find because they were exactly where Amy had said they would be. However, the belt for the mauve dress took time to discover, while the pearl brooch also remained elusive until it gleamed at her from a handkerchief drawer.

At last she closed the case, deciding to carry it downstairs where she would await Lucas's return. It seemed obvious that he would prefer to find her downstairs—and away from the vicinity of his bedroom, nor had she any wish to loiter in that particular locality. Oh no, she would never set foot in it again!

Yet despite her determined resolve she was unable to pass the door, and, almost as if drawn by an unseen force, she walked into the room which held such poignant memories for her.

As she gazed about her, the striped pyjamas thrown carelessly over a chair caused a wave of loving tenderness to surface and waft towards the absent Lucas, and then the rumpled unmade bed made her wonder why he was such a restless sleeper. The cover on the floor stirred her instinct for orderliness, and she knew she couldn't leave the bed in such a state.

Without thinking twice about the task she set the suitcase down and began to make the bed. Blanket corners were tucked in neatly, and she was putting the pillows in position when a woman's voice spoke from the doorway. Startled, she looked over her shoulder to see Maureen Ransom glaring at her.

Maureen came further into the room. 'What are you doing here?' she demanded icily.

Sylvia forced herself to smile. 'Making a bed—as you can see.'

'Lucas's bed, no doubt?'

'Yes, this is his room.' Why was Maureen here? Sylvia wondered, then added, 'If you've come to see him I'm afraid he's not here. He's at the office collecting letters to be posted.'

'I haven't come to see him. Actually, I've come to see his aunt, Mrs Grayson. I understand she's to be home this morning. I knocked on a door that opens into the kitchen, but there was no reply, so I walked in and came upstairs. Which is her room?'

Sylvia licked dry lips, instinct warning that trouble was about to loom. 'It's the next to the right.'

Maureen left her to go to the neighbouring room, but was back almost immediately. 'She's not there. Where is she?'

'In Sophia Street. She decided to have a few extra days with my mother. She's still very shaky.'

'Why didn't you say so at once?'

'You hadn't actually asked for her whereabouts.'

Maureen watched as Sylvia lifted the wide bedspread from the floor, but gave no assistance in adjusting it across the double bed. Suspicion began to glitter in her eyes as she demanded aggressively, 'Why are you making this bed?'

'Because it's unable to do the job for itself.'

'Don't you get smart with me!'

Sylvia made no reply. She moved to take Lucas's pyjamas from the chair, and after folding them neatly she placed them on one of the pillows.

Maureen's lips became a thin line. 'So he sleeps on that side of the bed?'

Sylvia shrugged, a light laugh escaping her as she said, 'How would I know?'

'Of course you know!' The words were hissed. 'You know because you slept with him last night. That's why you're here. It's why you're making the bed. His aunt's absence has given you a wonderful opportunity!'

Sylvia's cheeks flushed with anger as she snapped, 'Don't be ridiculous! It's not like that at all.'

'Isn't it? I'll bet it is.' Maureen stared at the suitcase, her irritation becoming more intense. 'Don't try to tell me I'm wrong. If I open that case I'll bet I'll find your sponge-bag and nightie—that's if you even wore one, which I doubt.' Her voice began to shake as it rose angrily. 'How long has this been going on?'

'Could that be your business?' retorted Sylvia, making an effort to control her own steadily mounting fury.

'It could be very much my business, considering the discussion I'm to have with Amy Grayson,' Maureen declared loftily.

'So Brian has talked. He couldn't keep his mouth shut.' The knowledge did nothing to subdue Sylvia's irritation.

'Never mind about Brian. If what I've heard is true I won't have someone like you coming between the boss and me. Tell me, *did you go to bed with him*?'

'Jealousy will get you nowhere.' Sylvia was unable to resist the taunt as she moved to straighten the disarray of articles on the dressing-table.

The words and the action served only to infuriate Maureen further. She moved swiftly to stand beside Sylvia, then, losing her temper, she hissed through clenched teeth, 'You blonde bitch, you *have* been to bed with him! I'll fix your flaxen hair for you!'

One hand grabbed a fistful of Sylvia's hair while the other snatched up a long-handled clothes brush which lay on the dressing-table. It rose in the air before landing with a cruel thud on Sylvia's head.

Taken unawares, she screamed as her hands went up to protect her head while trying to wrench her hair from Maureen's firm grasp. But the latter had now lost all control as she beat at Sylvia while shouting, 'Take that—and that—and that—*blonde bitch*!'

More screams escaped Sylvia as she struggled against the onslaught, but suddenly their vibrations were joined by a roar of fury from Lucas, who had arrived in time to witness the scene. He strode forward to grab Maureen's arm in a grip that caused her to yelp with pain as she tried to jerk it free.

'What's going on?' he gritted.

Maureen gaped at him speechlessly, while Sylvia collapsed against the dressing-table, where she held her head with both hands. Sobs escaped her while tears rolled down her cheeks.

Lucas continued to glare at Maureen. 'Well? I'm waiting to hear what this is all about.'

Maureen snapped defiantly, 'I was teaching her a lesson!'

Lucas frowned. 'What the devil are you talking about?'

'She—she has plans to trap you.'

'You must be round the bend! How could she possibly do that?'

'By getting you into bed, of course. What else could she have in mind? It's the oldest trick in the book.'

'Sylvia admitted this to you?' The question came softly.

'Not exactly, but neither am I blind. I can see the signs.'

'So you were belting the living daylights out of her on account of the signs you can see.'

Maureen betrayed a hint of nervousness. 'I—I'm afraid I lost my temper. I don't know what came over me.' She took a few steps towards Sylvia. 'I'm sorry, I didn't mean to hurt you, Sylvia. Let's forget it and be friends.'

'Forget it?' Sylvia cringed away from her. She had no wish for any further contact with Maureen.

The latter pressed fingers to her eyes as she attempted to make excuses for her vicious attack. 'It's all a blur. I can't even remember what made me become so upset.'

Lucas's voice came coldly. 'Perhaps you can remember what brought you to this house this morning.'

'Oh, yes. I came to see Mrs Grayson. I need to discuss something I've heard. Brian told me she'd be home this morning.'

'Ah, Brookes told you,' Lucas echoed. 'What other news did Brookes have for you? No doubt it was interesting.'

Maureen hesitated, then admitted, 'He wasn't very specific, but it was something about a partnership your aunt has in mind. I can only presume she told his mother about it. He advised me to talk to Mrs Grayson, so I came this morning. But she wasn't here. Instead I found *her*—making your bed.' She glared at Sylvia.

'And you presumed she'd just stepped out of it,' Lucas drawled.

Maureen nodded, then looked at him expectantly. 'Perhaps you can tell me about this—this other business.'

'Yes, I can enlighten you. My aunt has become bitten by the idea that I should take a partner, and I've decided to do so.'

Maureen's eyes shone. 'You have? How—how marvellous!'

'Naturally, the type of partner Amy has in mind is a wife, so you can be the first to learn that Sylvia and I are to be married.' He paused before adding wickedly, 'So instead of having just stepped out of my bed, she's about to step into it.'

Maureen's jaw sagged, then her lips curled. 'So she *has* trapped you!'

'And very nicely, thank you. It's a trap from which I've no wish to escape.'

Sylvia's eyes widened as she listened to his words in a daze of disbelief. She was aware that he had moved to her side and that his arms were now around her, holding her to his chest. Her head resting against his shoulder still ached from the pain of Maureen's blows, but somehow it didn't seem to matter.

Nor was this the type of proposal she had hoped for, or expected. Not that she had expected a proposal of any sort from Lucas, but that didn't matter either. What *did* matter was that he had said they were to be married, and suddenly her cup was as full as her eyes from which the tears brimmed and then fell.

But they were tears of joy and she could only put her arms about his waist while they soaked into his jacket. Then she caught her breath as Lucas uttered more words above her head.

'Ours will be more than a marriage partnership,' he told Maureen. 'I've decided that Sylvia and I will also hold a business arrangement. I know she'll soon gain your efficiency.'

'I suppose all—*this*—means you'll dispense with my services,' Maureen exclaimed bitterly.

'That will depend on Sylvia, and whether or not she's able to forget this morning's attack,' Lucas told her in a hard voice. 'It might upset her to see you around the place, and, as you yourself reminded her on Mokoia, nobody is indispensable.'

Sylvia spoke quickly. 'Let's forget the whole incident, Maureen. You have a good job with Lucas and there's no need for you to lose it.'

'You mean that?' Maureen's voice echoed with relief.

'Of course. Now if you'll please leave us I'd like to be alone with—with my future husband.'

Maureen turned swiftly to leave the room, but in doing so she almost fell over the suitcase which had been left near the door. The jolt she gave it unlatched its weak catch, causing the lid to flop open and the contents to spill. 'Sorry,' she muttered, and bent to push the garments back into the case.

Sylvia spoke in a clear cool tone. 'I've collected them for Amy. I trust you'll notice there's not a *nightie* or *sponge-bag*?'

'OK, I get the point,' Maureen conceded as she disappeared through the door.

Her departure was the signal for Lucas to hold Sylvia even closer. He kissed her deeply, then, looking down into her eyes, he said, 'Darling, I love you. I've never got you out of my system.'

'And I love you,' she whispered, gazing up at him.

'Say it again,' he pleaded. 'I've waited seven years to hear those words. Say you'll marry me!'

'I love you—I love you—I love you,' she breathed against his lips. 'Of course I'll marry you!'

He kissed her brow, her closed lids, her cheeks, then murmured huskily, 'Can we be married soon? I can't wait too long, darling.'

She nodded happily. 'Oh, yes—as soon as possible. Would you believe I was so sure you didn't want me to stay near you, that you wanted me out of the office?'

'What gave you that daft idea?'

'I've been longing for you to say you didn't want me to leave, but not a word did you utter,' Sylvia reproached him.

'Dearest, I've been searching for a sign to indicate that you wanted to stay in the job. I saw none. I didn't want you to stay simply because I *asked* you to. It had to be because you *wanted* to do so. And then, when I felt a little more sure——'

'Yes?' She looked at him wonderingly.

'Well, I intended taking you to Waiotapu, back to the Bridal Veil Falls, to ask you again. However, the sight of Maureen hammering at you with that clothes brush made me see red, and I jumped the gun.'

'The result is worth the pain,' she admitted shyly, thrilling to the feel of his hand holding her breast.

'I fear she could have really hurt you.' His hand moved to smooth her hair, and although his touch was gentle her wince caused him to investigate further. 'My oath, you have real bumps on your head!'

'Yes—they're somewhat tender,' Sylvia admitted.

'Yet you told Maureen you're willing to forget the affair. Well, I'm not,' he declared wrathfully. 'She'll have to go.'

'But, darling, there's so much work to be done. The office needs her——'

'The office needs her like you need these bumps on your head, and that's not at all. Every time I look at her I'll see her attacking you, and that's something I'll not tolerate. In any case, we've already managed without her, or have you forgotten what brought you back to me?'

'How could I forget? It was her absence due to the 'flu.' Sylvia looked at him anxiously. 'You're quite determined about this?'

'Definitely. I had no idea she'd belted you to such an extent.'

'She got a few whacks in before you arrived.' Secretly she felt relieved. The office would be a happier place without Maureen, and after all, whether or not she remained in the place was Lucas's decision.

He kissed her again, long and tenderly, until he said, 'Darling, there's so much to do, so much to plan, but if we don't leave this room I'll carry you to that bed.'

She hid her face against him lest he read the truth in her eyes. Her entire body felt weak and pliable with longing to respond, and once on the bed she knew she would be unable to resist him.

He said, 'Something tells me you'd prefer to wait.'

She nodded. 'We'll make up for it later—I promise.'

'With wanton abandon?'

His mouth claimed hers in a demanding kiss that betrayed the depth of his yearning to make love. Then his hands on her shoulders put her from him, firmly and decisively. 'Now for action,' he declared. 'First we must take Amy's clothes to her. She'll be glad to know that I now agree with her partnership plan.'

'And that's it signed and sealed with our love,' Sylvia added.

Lucas said, 'This afternoon we must go to Mokoia. That little old fellow Matua Tonga must be thanked for granting my wish.'

Sylvia's eyes widened in amazement. 'You wished for this?'

'Of course. I've been wishing for it for seven years. I should have consulted him ages ago. He's not as dumb as he looks.'

Sylvia began to laugh. 'Yes, let's go to Mokoia. I also owe him gratitude.'

Lucas's brows rose. 'Are you saying that you also wished for this? Standing hand in hand, did we wish for the same thing?'

'It seems to be the case. I realised it was what I wanted above all else in the world, but I had no idea that you were making the same wish.'

'So let's go. He's sure to be expecting a progress report.' He snatched up the suitcase and carried it downstairs.

Sylvia followed him happily, knowing she would be content to follow him from this day forward. She sat in a blissful daze as the car sped along Fenton Street, and as he pulled up in the driveway Lucas asked a question that made things seem even more unreal.

'How would Hawaii suit you for a honeymoon?'

'*Hawaii?* Wonderful! But only if you're with me,' Sylvia added, dreamily.

'What makes you imagine you'd be allowed there without me?' he teased.

When they went inside Ruth and Amy were delighted with their news. Heads together, they began planning the wedding at once.

Lucas put his arms round Sylvia. 'Are you happy, my darling?'

She nodded. 'I'm in a whirl. I'm afraid I'll wake up.'

He kissed her deeply. 'It's not a dream, beloved. It's only the beginning of our life together.' He paused, frowning. 'Do you know, I've a strong suspicion that Amy imagines this is all her doing.'

Sylvia suppressed a smile. 'Dear Amy, I love her almost as much as I love Mother——'

Further words were impossible as Lucas's lips again found her own.

PASSPORT TO ROMANCE VACATION SWEEPSTAKES

OFFICIAL RULES

SWEEPSTAKES RULES AND REGULATIONS. NO PURCHASE NECESSARY.

HOW TO ENTER:

1. To enter, complete this official entry form and return with your invoice in the envelope provided, or print your name, address, telephone number and age on a plain piece of paper and mail to: Passport to Romance, P.O. Box #1397, Buffalo, N.Y. 14269-1397. No mechanically reproduced entries accepted.
2. All entries must be received by the Contest Closing Date, midnight, December 31, 1990 to be eligible.
3. Prizes: There will be ten (10) Grand Prizes awarded, each consisting of a choice of a trip for two people to: i) London, England (approximate retail value $5,050 U.S.); ii) England, Wales and Scotland (approximate retail value $6,400 U.S.); iii) Caribbean Cruise (approximate retail value $7,300 U.S.); iv) Hawaii (approximate retail value $ 9,550 U.S.); v) Greek Island Cruise in the Mediterranean (approximate retail value $12,250 U.S.); vi) France (approximate retail value $7,300 U.S.).
4. Any winner may choose to receive any trip or a cash alternative prize of $5,000.00 U.S. in lieu of the trip.
5. Odds of winning depend on number of entries received.
6. A random draw will be made by Nielsen Promotion Services, an independent judging organization on January 29, 1991, in Buffalo, N.Y., at 11:30 a.m. from all eligible entries received on or before the Contest Closing Date. Any Canadian entrants who are selected must correctly answer a time-limited, mathematical skill-testing question in order to win. Quebec residents may submit any litigation respecting the conduct and awarding of a prize in this contest to the Régie des loteries et courses du Quebec.
7. Full contest rules may be obtained by sending a stamped, self-addressed envelope to: "Passport to Romance Rules Request", P.O. Box 9998, Saint John, New Brunswick, E2L 4N4.
8. Payment of taxes other than air and hotel taxes is the sole responsibility of the winner.
9. Void where prohibited by law.

PASSPORT TO ROMANCE VACATION SWEEPSTAKES

OFFICIAL RULES

SWEEPSTAKES RULES AND REGULATIONS. NO PURCHASE NECESSARY.

HOW TO ENTER:

1. To enter, complete this official entry form and return with your invoice in the envelope provided, or print your name, address, telephone number and age on a plain piece of paper and mail to: Passport to Romance, P.O. Box #1397, Buffalo, N.Y. 14269-1397. No mechanically reproduced entries accepted.
2. All entries must be received by the Contest Closing Date, midnight, December 31, 1990 to be eligible.
3. Prizes: There will be ten (10) Grand Prizes awarded, each consisting of a choice of a trip for two people to: i) London, England (approximate retail value $5,050 U.S.); ii) England, Wales and Scotland (approximate retail value $6,400 U.S.); iii) Caribbean Cruise (approximate retail value $7,300 U.S.); iv) Hawaii (approximate retail value $ 9,550 U.S.); v) Greek Island Cruise in the Mediterranean (approximate retail value $12,250 U.S.); vi) France (approximate retail value $7,300 U.S.).
4. Any winner may choose to receive any trip or a cash alternative prize of $5,000.00 U.S. in lieu of the trip.
5. Odds of winning depend on number of entries received.
6. A random draw will be made by Nielsen Promotion Services, an independent judging organization on January 29, 1991, in Buffalo, N.Y., at 11:30 a.m. from all eligible entries received on or before the Contest Closing Date. Any Canadian entrants who are selected must correctly answer a time-limited, mathematical skill-testing question in order to win. Quebec residents may submit any litigation respecting the conduct and awarding of a prize in this contest to the Régie des loteries et courses du Quebec.
7. Full contest rules may be obtained by sending a stamped, self-addressed envelope to: "Passport to Romance Rules Request", P.O. Box 9998, Saint John, New Brunswick, E2L 4N4.
8. Payment of taxes other than air and hotel taxes is the sole responsibility of the winner.
9. Void where prohibited by law.

 RLS-DIR

VACATION SWEEPSTAKES

MONTH 2 ENTRY

Official Entry Form

Yes, enter me in the drawing for one of ten Vacations-for-Two! If I'm a winner, I'll get my choice of any of the six different destinations being offered — and I won't have to decide until after I'm notified!

Return entries with invoice in envelope provided along with Daily Travel Allowance Voucher. Each book in your shipment has two entry forms — and the more you enter, the better your chance of winning!

Name

Address Apt.

City State/Prov. Zip/Postal Code

Daytime phone number ____________
Area Code

☐ I am enclosing a Daily Travel Allowance Voucher in the amount of $__________ Write in amount revealed beneath scratch-off

VACATION SWEEPSTAKES

MONTH 2 ENTRY

Official Entry Form

Yes, enter me in the drawing for one of ten Vacations-for-Two! If I'm a winner, I'll get my choice of any of the six different destinations being offered — and I won't have to decide until after I'm notified!

Return entries with invoice in envelope provided along with Daily Travel Allowance Voucher. Each book in your shipment has two entry forms — and the more you enter, the better your chance of winning!

Name

Address Apt.

City State/Prov. Zip/Postal Code

Daytime phone number ____________
Area Code

☐ I am enclosing a Daily Travel Allowance Voucher in the amount of $__________ Write in amount revealed beneath scratch-off

CPS-TWO